STORIES
TO
TREASURE

Illustrated by Eric Kincaid

BRIMAX BOOKS • NEWMARKET • ENGLAND

Introduction

This is a collection of original stories and poems that children will love.

Open the pages and you step into a fairytale world of friendly dragons and mad inventors, foolish kings and beautiful princesses, kindly giants and naughty elves, grumpy witches and bumbling wizards. You will even meet a pig that can fly!

All of them have their own story to tell. Some are happy, some are sad. Some are funny, some are silly. They are all beautifuly illustrated by Eric Kincaid. Together, the stories and pictures will catch you in their magic spell. They will make you want to return to them again and again as stories to treasure.

Contents

THE DRAGON OF DUMBY

The citizens of Dumby were worried. Every week one of their enemies attacked them.

"What we need is a dragon," said the Mayor. "A big, fierce dragon."

"We did have one, a long time ago," mumbled old Mr Snoddy. "But he grew old and useless, like me. We never replaced him. Expensive monsters, dragons."

"We could get one from the Wildlife Dragon Park," said the Mayor. So he sent a telegram. Early next morning, he had a reply. It read:

GOOD QUALITY DRAGON ARRIVING AT TEN O'CLOCK. DO NOT OVERFEED HIM. CAN BE EXCHANGED IF UNSATISFACTORY.

As the city clock chimed ten, a long, narrow cart rattled into the cobbled square. Inside was a long, narrow dragon.

The mayor stepped forward to make a speech of welcome, as the dragon clambered out of the cart, wagging his tail. The Mayor was taken aback. "You should look much fiercer than that!" he exclaimed.

The dragon looked surprised. "I'm not fierce at all!" he said, in a jolly voice.

The children were delighted with the dragon. They crowded round, touching his scaly green skin.

"You're not as big as we expected," said Pip, the baker's son.

The dragon looked wistful. "I'd like to be bigger," he said, "but dragons come in different sizes, just like people."

"What's your name?" asked one of the children.

The dragon looked bashful. "Promise you won't laugh," he said. Everyone promised. "It's Dermot," he went on, "but I'd rather be called Fred."

"Nonsense!" said the Mayor briskly. "Fred's no name for a dragon—it wouldn't frighten a fly! Dermot you're called, and Dermot you'll stay."

He looked the dragon over. "What do you eat?" he asked.

Dermot licked his lips. "Cucumber," he said. "Celery, and rhubarb."

The Mayor groaned. "All long, thin food!" he said. "No wonder you're *that* shape."

So Dermot was put on a 'round' diet; melons, pumpkins, dumplings, and Christmas puddings. One day he even swallowed Pip's football by mistake. He doubled his size in less than a week.

"That's better," said the Mayor. "Now, are you good at puffing smoke?"

Dermot hung his head. "Didn't they tell you? I was always bottom of the smoke-puffing class."

The Mayor was worried. What was the use of a dragon who couldn't puff? He began to think seriously of asking for an exchange dragon.

Early next morning, Billy the Bugler, who'd been on night patrol, sounded the alert.

Dermot, who slept in a railway tunnel because it was the same shape as himself, woke with a start. The Mayor snatched off his nightcap and jumped out of bed. "It's the Bandidados—they always attack on Tuesdays!" he cried.

Captain Beat-e-moff was giving orders to Dumby's small army. "Push out the cannon!" he shouted.

The cannon creaked, squeaked, and wobbled.

"Can't you oil it?" said the Mayor irritably.

"Sorry," said the Captain. "But the King wanted the oil for his armour."

His Majesty tottered out of the Palace, calling in a quavery voice: "Where's my good old Dando?"

Dando was brought from his stable, wearing his shabby old saddle.

"Don't forget his glasses!" said the King. "He can't see the enemy without them!"

It took five soldiers to heave His Majesty onto Dando's back.

"Where's the new dragon?" quavered the King. "He must come in front with me."

Dermot groaned. Fighting was such a silly waste of time, but he would have to do his best. The people of Dumby had given him a home—he must try and repay them.

The procession moved out of the city gate. The King wobbled so much that his armour rattled. The enemy came in sight. A hundred fierce Bandidados, wearing their red helmets with green feathers at the side. In front was the biggest, fiercest dragon Dermot had ever seen. Smoke poured from his nostrils, and he was roaring in fine style.

The King looked down at Dermot. "We haven't got a chance against this lot, have we, dragon?" he quavered.

Dermot shook his head in despair. Then he took a deep breath. Making a great effort, he managed to puff a very small cloud of smoke.

"I did it!" he shouted. He went on puffing. The clouds got bigger.

Captain Beat-e-moff was delighted. "Dragon – forward – CHARGE!" he yelled.

Dermot rushed forward. Soon the Bandidados and their dragon were struggling in a thick fog of smoke. Then Captain Beat-e-moff sent Billy the Bugler round behind the enemy. When he sounded the attack, the Bandidados thought the Dumby army was behind them. They turned and rushed off down the hill.

Dermot was a hero.

"I knew you could do it if you tried!" beamed the Mayor, crossing Tuesday off the calendar. "Now just keep in practice for Thursday, young Dermot. That's when we expect the Black Baron and his Boldos. They're a *very* nasty crowd."

But early next morning there was a shout from Captain Beat-e-moff. "Enemy in sight!" he yelled.

"It's not even Thursday!" gasped the Mayor.

Dermot's heart sank. He hoped his puff was in good order.

"Never mind about the King," shouted the Captain. "There's no time to get him mounted. Come along, young dragon-me-lad!"

The Boldos, looking very villainous, were already half way across Dumby Marsh. In front was an enormous, roaring dragon.

Poor Dermot was terrified. *His* smoke would be little use against such a monster. How he wished he was back at the Wildlife Park!

Then an amazing thing happened. The enemy dragon stopped, and stared. "Dermot!" he roared, a broad grin spreading across his huge scaly face.

"Cyril!" squeaked Dermot, running forward.

The two armies were so surprised that they sat down to watch.

"When did you leave the Wildlife Park?" asked Cyril.

Dermot told him everything.

"I'm at Morrogan," said Cyril. "They're not a bad lot, but they will keep fighting! I put on a show to please them, but I do wish they'd give it up."

"So do I!" Dermot was delighted that Cyril felt the same.

"Why don't we start a Peaceful Dragon Club?" said Cyril.

So they did. In less than a week every dragon for miles around had joined. So there was no more fighting.

The citizens of Dumby were delighted, and very proud of Dermot.

As Pip said: "He may *look* big and fierce, but inside he's the gentlest dragon in the world!"

So the Mayor sent a telegram to the Wildlife Park. It read: "Completely satisfied with good quality dragon. Do *not* wish to exchange."

SPOTTY POTTY

Percy Potamus said "Oh whatamus
Am I going to do today?
On my tum there are some spotamus,
Not just a few but rather a lotamus.
In my bed I think I'll stay.
My head is aching, I feel hotamus,
Now I see there are spots on my poor
botamus!
Oh, I am a poorly Potamus,
Wish my spots would go away."

His Mother Mrs. Hippy Potamus
Said "German Measles is what you've
gotamus,
I'll bring your breakfast on a tray.
Tomorrow those spots will be only
dotamus,
You'll feel better and want to play."

THE HOUSE THAT JACK BUILT

This is the house that Jack built.

This is the tree
As you can see
That grew through the floor
And what is more
Grew right through the house that Jack built.

18

This is the rook
That came to look
To build his nest
His first and best
Up in the tree
As you can see
That grew through the floor
And what is more
Grew right through the house that Jack built.

This is his wife
Who shares his life
High in the nest
His first and best
Up in the tree
As you can see
That grew through the floor
And what is more
Grew right through the house that Jack built.

Here are their eggs
Safe in the nest
Their first and best
Up in the tree
As you can see
That grew through the floor
And what is more
Grew right through the house that Jack built.

"Our babies are hungry!"
  Mother Rook sings;
So, Father brings meals –
How happy he feels
And proud of his wife
Who shares his life
High in the nest
His first and best
Up in the tree
As you can see
That grew through the floor
And what is more
Grew right through the house that Jack built.

Caws never cease
As rooks increase
A real busy sound
And babies abound
Each from an egg
Their mouths all beg;
Husbands help wives
Who share their lives
High in each nest
Their first and best
Up in the tree
As you can see
That grew through the floor
And what is more
Grew right through the house that Jack built.

20

Jack calls his house
'The Rookery-Nook'
It's famous and so
He's writing a book.
Folks come by car
They come by plane;
They see it once
Then come again.
If the tree grows bigger,
Somebody said,
You'll never climb
Those stairs to bed!
Cut it down now!
That is the best!
'Good gracious!' thought Jack,
'And spoil each nest!
Never! No, never!
Not on your life!
I'll search and find
Myself a wife;
We'll stay right here
High up in the house that Jack built.'

Now Jack has a 'nest'
His first and best
He is happy
As happy can be
There with his wife
Who shares his life
High up in the tree
As you can see
That grew through the floor
And what is more
Grew right through the house that Jack built.

ALVIN'S QUEST

Of all the animals in Africa, Alvin the Aardvark was the most humble. He knew that the other animals thought him ugly and odd, with his bald tail, big ears and funny eating habits. So when he returned home just before dawn, covered in earth but pleasantly full of tasty, tickly ants, he was surprised to find a note pinned to his burrow door.

Dear Alvin, read the note, *I wish you to discover who is first among all the animals. I shall return tonight for your answer. The Lord of All Animals.*

Alvin was, to say the least, very surprised. He knew that the Lord of All Animals was fond of giving his subjects tasks to do. However, he never dreamed that such an unimportant creature as himself would ever be chosen.

'Oh my goodness!' thought Alvin. 'He wants my answer by tonight!'

By this time, the sun was coming up over the mountains and Alvin was feeling that it was time for bed. Aardvarks are night animals, and Alvin had had a very busy night digging out a particularly large (and delicious!) nest of white termites. He was full; he was tired; he needed his sleep.

'By tonight!' thought Alvin again, a little more crossly this time, and he waddled off back into the jungle to think deeply.

Now Aardvarks are not only odd-looking animals, but they are not very bright. The very worst time of all for a not-very-bright Aardvark to do some deep thinking is nine o'clock on a hot morning when he should be curled up fast asleep.

By ten o'clock Alvin had nodded off three times, and was no nearer to working out who was first of all the animals. He was just dozing off for the fourth time, when slithering along the jungle path came Boris the Boa-Constrictor.

It was probably just as well for Alvin that Boris too, was full of breakfast, otherwise Alvin might never have found the answer. As it was, Boris was so surprised to see an Aardvark sitting in the middle of a jungle path in the middle of the morning, that most of him slid to a very sudden stop.

"Well, well!" he sighed, in a soft voice that sent shivers right to the tip of Alvin's hairless tail. "What have we here?"

'P-please," stammered Alvin, "it's only me, Alvin the Aardvark. The Lord of All Animals has sent me to discover who is first of all the animals. The trouble is I don't know where to start."

The big snake laughed silently, his smooth, scaly skin rippling with amusement. "You are fortunate, little friend," he breathed, "for you have found him."

"Who?" squeaked Alvin. "Er, who?" he repeated in a firmer voice, trying not to let Boris see his fear.

"Why, the first of all the animals!" rasped Boris, a little crossly. "Which creature is longer than I? Or more beautiful?" he added, looking back at his patterned coils admiringly. When he looked back again, Alvin had completely disappeared . . . . . .

All the world seemed to be asleep as Alvin dragged his hot and thirsty body out of the shelter of the jungle into the glare of the midday sun. "Boris is the longest of the Lord's animals," he thought aloud, "but does that make him the first?"

"Of course not!" boomed a voice so loud that Alvin tumbled backwards head-over-heels with fright. "I am!"

Alvin found himself looking very closely at what appeared to be a grey, wrinkled tree trunk. In fact it was a leg, a leg attached to a large and very proud-looking elephant.

"Oh, it's you, Ernest!" sighed Alvin.

"It is indeed," trumpeted Ernest, "and it is quite obvious that the Lord meant me. I am the biggest and heaviest of all the creatures so *I* must be the first."

"Oh! Yes! Quite! Thank you, Ernest," mumbled Alvin, but a little nagging voice inside his narrow, pointed head kept repeating, "Not the longest, not the heaviest, but the first." Sighing, he set off deeper into the plain.

By the time he came to a water-hole, Alvin was even more confused. Colin the Cheetah had told him as he zoomed past at full speed that HE must be first because he was the fastest. Gordon the Giraffe had grunted down to him that HE must be the first, being the tallest of the Lord's animals. But still Alvin told himself, "The Lord said 'the FIRST', not the longest, heaviest, fastest or tallest. What COULD he have meant? Who could it be?"

Alvin was sitting on a log, sipping up warm, muddy but quite refreshing water with his long pink tongue. Then the log spoke.

"It is me," it said, in a deep, bubbly voice.

"Who was that?" enquired Alvin, looking all around and seeing no one.

"Me," said the log again. "Caspar."

"Oh, it's YOU!" cried Alvin, scuttling quickly back to the soggy-but-safe bank. The crocodile's mouth gaped open in a snaggle-toothed smile.

"Look at my scales!" he burbled. "See how hard and bright they are. I am the only one of the Lord's animals with such tough and beautiful armour. I am the toughest, therefore *I* must be the first."

Even an Aardvark, with claws like long, curved knives, does not argue with a crocodile, especially a conceited one.

Alvin bumbled away again, but he was still not sure. "The longest, the heaviest, the fastest, the tallest and now the toughest," he said to himself. "Which of them is the first of all the Lord's animals?"

Doubtfully, Alvin wandered homewards over the dry, dusty, sun-scorched plain. Without warning, a small but piercing whisper stopped him dead in his tracks. "Halt or you die!" It was Scarletta the Scorpion, as she lay, sting upraised, in the shadow of Alvin's right forefoot!

"I have no quarrel with you, Scarletta!" gasped Alvin. Nor has anyone with any sense, he thought. "I have been sent by the Lord of All Animals to find out who is first of all the animals. Have you any idea?"

Scarletta took a long time to answer and Alvin's leg was getting rather cramped. There was a wicked little glitter in her eye as she spoke. "I will give you a clue," she said. "Which creature is the only one that can kill an animal many times bigger than itself?"

Alvin looked down at the evil, poisonous hook quivering on the end of Scarletta's tail. He looked at his poor cramped foot just above it. "You?" he suggested.

"Exactly," whispered Scarletta. "I am the deadliest. Therefore, *I* am the first of all the animals."

With that she disappeared beneath a large, flat stone.

Alvin limped slowly but gratefully back towards the edge of the jungle. His stomach was rumbling. He turned to look at a mouth-watering ant heap and was wondering if he had time for a snack, when he bumped into something large, warm, furry and cross.

If you have ever been awakened from a delightful dream by being trodden on by a careless Aardvark, you will understand how Leroy felt. Leroy was the local lion and he was used to being treated with respect. He was *not* used to being trampled on.

"Watch where you're going, you aimless Aardvark!" he snarled sleepily.

"I'm terribly sorry, Leroy," apologised Alvin. "I was thinking about something."

"I'll bet that was the first time," replied Leroy, nastily. Well, he had just been woken up. "I hope," he said, looking at Alvin and wondering how Aardvark tasted, "that this thought was important enough to be worth disturbing my sleep." Lions can be very bad-tempered and big-headed.

"Perhaps you can help me?" asked Alvin, tactfully changing the subject. "The Lord of All Animals has told me to find out who is first of all animals. He wants my answer by tonight and it's late already and everybody I've met thinks they are the first." He waited breathlessly for Leroy to reply.

"You silly little creature," sniffed Leroy. "Who is King of the Jungle?"

"Why, you of course!" replied Alvin quickly.

"Well then, that answers your question!" snapped Leroy. "And now, if you don't mind . . . . . ." He flopped back onto his side and fell asleep. He had decided that Aardvarks looked tough and stringy and that anything that ate ANTS was not fit for a lion's dinner.

"The Lord said FIRST," Alvin repeated stubbornly to himself as he went slowly back into the jungle.

"The first WHAT, kid?" hooted a voice from far above. A storm of banana skins and peanut shells broke over Alvin's head. Then a large, brown, furry shape thudded softly to the ground just in front of him. It was Cardew the Chimpanzee.

Alvin told Cardew the whole story.

"Your problems are over, kid. He must mean ME," chuckled Cardew, scratching comfortably.

"Why? Er, with respect," added Alvin, as Cardew's eyes narrowed into a mean expression.

"I'm the first, 'cause I'm the cleverest, that's why!" chattered Cardew. "Of course, what would an AARDVARK know about intelligence?" he added, seeing Alvin's doubtful expression. "Ant-grubber! Bare-tail!" His insults faded as he swung away through the trees. "Call yourself an animal . . ."

Alvin was worried. It was nearly dark, he was nearing home, how sore his feet were! – and he still didn't know which animal was first. He knew which was the longest, the heaviest, the fastest, the tallest, the toughest, the deadliest, the proudest and the most intelligent. But which was the first?

It was then that he saw the man. He was dressed all in white, with a funny round hat and had a kind, red face. Blue eyes twinkled through thick spectacles. The man also saw Alvin. ''An Aardvark!'' he cried, jumping to his feet and waving a camera at Alvin. ''An Aardvark – look!'' He pointed to a large, colour photograph in a book by his side.

''Yes, I'm an Aardvark,'' replied Alvin grumpily. ''What's so exciting about that? I'm not the longest or heaviest or fastest or tallest or toughest or deadliest or proudest animal. And I'm certainly not the most intelligent,'' he added sadly.

''Never mind, little Aardvark,'' smiled the man kindly.

''You are the first . . . ''

''WHAT!'' yelped Alvin, nearly knocking the poor man off his feet.

''*I* am the first?''

"Certainly!" replied the red-faced little man. "Look in my animal book." Then he took Alvin's picture and explained that he had come to Africa to photograph all the animals in order from A-Z. Had Alvin any idea where he might find a baboon? But Alvin had gone, reaching the door of his burrow just as the last of the sun went down below the mountain tops.

"You see, Alvin," said a voice, deep as a well and soothing as syrup. "You may not be as long, or as heavy or as fast or as tall or tough or deadly or proud or even clever, but in one way you are first. Your name would come first in an animal alphabet. All my animals are different, yet I love them all. So in his own way, each one is first. Just like you, Alvin."

But Alvin was already fast asleep, dreaming of delicious, crunchy, tickly ants . . . .

WYNKEN, BLYNKEN, AND NOD

Wynken, Blynken, and Nod one night
   Sailed off in a wooden shoe, –
Sailed on a river of misty light
   Into a sea of dew.
"Where are you going, and what do you wish?"
   The old moon asked the three.
"We have come to fish for the herring-fish
   That live in the beautiful sea;
Nets of silver and gold have we,"
   Said Wynken,
      Blynken,
      And Nod.

The old moon laughed and sung a song,
   As they rocked in the wooden shoe;
And the wind that sped them all night long
   Ruffled the waves of dew;
The little stars were the herring-fish
   That lived in the beautiful sea.
"Now cast your nets wherever you wish,
   But never afeared are we!"
So cried the stars to the fisherman three,
      Wynken,
      Blynken,
      And Nod.

All night long their nets they threw
    For the fish in the twinkling foam,
Then down the sky came the wooden shoe,
    Bringing the fishermen home;
'Twas all so pretty a sail, it seemed
    As if it could not be;
And some folk thought 'twas a dream they dreamed
    Of sailing that beautiful sea;
But I shall name you the fishermen three;
       Wynken,
       Blynken,
       And Nod.

Wynken and Blynken are two little eyes,
    And Nod is a little head,
And the wooden shoe that sailed the skies
    Is a wee one's single bed!
So shut your eyes while Mother sings
    Of wonderful sights that be,
And you shall see the beautiful things
    As you rock on the misty sea
Where the old shoe rocked the fishermen three,
       Wynken,
       Blynken,
       And Nod.

FELIX THE MAGICIAN

Long, long ago there lived a good and clever magician whose name was Felix. He lived on the border between two warlike countries. Felix knew that King Lofty on the one side and King Trump on the other were jealous of each other and needed little excuse to start a war.

Their armies trained by marching up hill and down dale all day long. Tramp, tramp, tramp.

Felix was cross.

"I must put a stop to it," he said to himself. But how?

Felix thought and thought. He even worried about it in his sleep.

"At last," he cried, jumping out of bed one night in his night-shirt and cap.

He searched through his spell books until he found what he was looking for, then he carried it upstairs with him and sat up in bed reading it carefully. Every now and then, he nodded and chuckled to himself, and at last, he lay down and went fast asleep.

Felix spent all the next day preparing and just before midnight he left the house making his way to the border. Luckily there was very little moonlight, but he had to go carefully not to be seen by one of the soldiers.

First, he stood facing one way and held up his arms chanting very quietly to himself. He turned and did the same thing facing the other way. Then he jumped smartly to one side and made his way home chuckling to himself.

The following morning he found he had just been in time. The soldiers were preparing themselves for battle. Rank upon rank were lined up facing each other. Felix was not smiling now. Thinking of all the dreadful things that would have happened if he had not cast his spell made him very angry.

On one side of the border, King Lofty stood near his white horse his captains grouped about him.

King Trump was already astride his black horse waiting for his officers to tell him they were ready.

There were only a few yards between the armies, but when Felix thought of those few yards he had to smile. He went out and sat on a large rock where he could see everything that was going on. He did not want to miss anything.

Felix had to admit they looked a wonderful sight lined up facing each other. The soldiers stood in ranks, their spears and shields glinting in the sun. Behind them the archers stood, their bows and arrows ready.

Now, both kings held their swords aloft ready to give a signal. Both arms came down almost at the same moment. The two armies marched towards each other, shields in place and spears ready. Both sides thrust their spears forward but they did not touch the men on the other side. Instead they buckled and snapped in half! The soldiers fell backwards in a heap. The same thing happened to the next rank and the one after.

By now the archers had started to let fly their arrows. These flew only so far in the air then fell harmlessly to the ground. Felix was enjoying himself, he laughed until the tears ran down his cheeks.

Some of the archers began to smile, then laugh; they could not help it. It was such a funny sight — all those arms and legs waving in the air.

King Lofty and King Trump looked stupidly at their men who kept marching forward and falling on top of the soldiers already on the ground. The laughter spread until even the two kings had to join in. At last, one of the officers gave the command to halt.

Felix waved his arms to take the invisible wall away. One of the soldiers noticed Felix sitting on the rock, and pointed to him. Everybody became silent looking towards him. King Lofty and King Trump rode up to him and dismounted. Seeing his hat and cloak they looked at each other.

"You did this," said King Lofty.

"Why?" asked King Trump.

"Yes, it was me," said Felix. "Why? Well, someone had to do something before you destroyed each other."

"How did you do it?" asked King Lofty.

"It was simple really,' said Felix. "I put an invisible wall between you."

Well, the kings were very impressed and said how clever he had been.

"Yes, I know that," said Felix modestly. "Come now," he went on.

"Shake hands and forget this war. It seems to me that you are both to blame."

The two kings looked at each other. Then they smiled and clasped hands. The soldiers cheered their kings, the officers and most of all Felix, the clever magician.

Felix was delighted his spell had worked. He invited both kings and their officers to his house to rest and talk. All the men of both sides joined together, laughing and clapping each other on the back.

Felix waved his arms, and food and drink appeared by magic. The men cheered once more, then they ate and drank until it was almost dark, before going home. There was so much to tell their families, they could hardly believe all the wonderful things that had happened that day.

Felix's name was on everyone's lips, and he was blessed that day and for many, many years to come.

BUMBLYWITCH

At the bottom of Farmer Tumlytod's field, in a cottage shaped like a honeypot, there lived a witch. She was both good and kind and her name was Bumblywitch. Her black cat was called Jet and he had green eyes. He was fond of Bumblywitch and took care of her.

"Meow Maroo," he would say to Bumblywitch, "I am near you."

On a different patch, in cottages of their own, lived Bumblywitch's two sisters, Grumblywitch and Fumblywitch. They got on well together and often met for a talk.

Bumblywitch liked doing things to help people when they were ill or had a problem. "Izzy Whizzy, must keep busy," she was always saying. Nothing was ever too much trouble. A simple magic spell, a herb potion, these things kept her busy and the days passed happily.

The bees in the hive in her garden would hum bits of news in her ear, "Old Henry's hens are not laying. Granny Granger's goose is straying," they buzzed at her. Animals and birds often came to the cottage too, to tell Bumblywitch when there were things that needed her attention.

There was always plenty of work to do.

There came a day when Bumblywitch had a problem of her own, she was getting too fat! She gave Jet his saucer of milk, sat down to put on her elastic-sided witch's boots and found they would not go on! It was impossible!

"Oh Fiddledeedee," cried poor Bumblywitch, "I know I love doughnuts and chocolate when I get a sinking feeling inside me and I enjoy hot buttered toast when I'm sitting in my comfortable chair by the fire and cups of hot sweet tea. Oh dear, Jet, do you think I could wear my best buckle shoes?" and she went to fetch them.

Jet watched her carefully. "Meow Maroo," he said, and thought to himself that Bumblywitch was indeed *much* rounder than she used to be.

Bumblywitch sat down again and tried to put on her best witch's buckle shoes, but they hurt her ankles.

"Bumblyberries, I shall have to go out in my slippers because I must go and gather some more herbs," she cried. "Oh this is terrible!"

Hoping that she would not meet another witch while she was wearing her slippers, Bumblywitch went out. She walked to a nearby hedge to look for more herbs to fill up her store in the cottage. Bending with difficulty over a rather wide ditch, poor Bumblywitch slipped and fell in headfirst. The ditch was watery and rather unpleasant. Some pigeons who were in a tree watching, sang unkindly,

"Poor Bumblywitch,
She fell in a ditch,
Couldn't get out,
She stuck, 'cos she's stout!"

41

Then the pigeons felt sorry and wanted to help her. Flying down from their tree, they took hold of her clothes in their beaks and gently pulled her out. Muddy and very short of breath, Bumblywitch saw that her tall, black hat was stuck in the bottom of the ditch.

"Toads and Newts," she said loudly, feeling how it was very very improper for a witch to be seen wearing slippers and without a hat as well. Two kind crows pulled her hat out of the ditch and put it back on her head, although it was a bit wet! It dripped muddy water down her face.

"Whatever would my sisters say if they could see me now. Just as well they live on a different patch," gasped Bumblywitch. It was all so funny that she began to laugh. She thanked the birds for helping her and, walking very carefully, went back to her little cottage.

"Meow Maree," said Jet when he met her at the cottage door, "Meow Maroo, what did you do?" He was upset because if he had been there, perhaps he could have stopped Bumblywitch from falling in the watery ditch.

Bumblywitch made some tea and hot buttered toast and poured out a large saucer of milk for Jet. After he had finished his milk, in between washing and purring, Jet told Bumblywitch that Widow Twitchett's cow Daisy was sick. At once she got to her feet and went to fetch her broomstick because she did feel a little tired.

"I won't be long," she said to Jet, "a little magic whispered in Daisy's large, soft ear will soon put that right." She would take over some ointment for Widow Twitchett's bad knees too. Taking her broomstick into the yard outside, Bumblywitch put her leg over it and sat down, saying,

"Broomstick, broomstick,

Now I'm ready.

Travel me quick,

Keep me steady."

At once, the broomstick whirred into action for take-off. There was a strange noise, clouds of dust rose from underneath, the handle of the broomstick rose slightly, but Bumblywitch did not!

What was happening now! The broomstick was trying so hard to move but he simply could not rise from the ground. Bumblywitch was far too heavy. Very cross and not a little upset, Bumblywitch tried stronger magic,

"Rise I say, up and away.

On the ground you shall not stay."

The broomstick rose from the ground for about twelve inches, then with a very loud bump, returned to the ground again. It was no good. For once in her life, kind Bumblywitch was angry and with herself. This was too much. First her boots and now her broomstick.

"You are in no way to blame," she told her broomstick, "this is all my fault." As she put him away in his usual corner, she decided what she must do. She must act at once. She must get thinner and she must do it quickly before the other witches found out.

No more doughnuts, no more chocolate (except on Saturday night) less butter on her toast and only a small spoonful of honey in her nightly hot drink.

As she was unable to ride her broomstick, she would have to walk everywhere and work twice as hard. Now she must begin by walking over to Widow Twitchett and Daisy the cow.

"Hocus Pocus," said Bumblywitch as she walked up hill and down hill. Luckily for her, as she was a witch, she was able to use a little simple magic for getting over stiles and awkward places. Otherwise, Bumblywitch walked everywhere. Her good friend Farmer Tumlytod grew quite concerned about her. Returning to her cottage, Bumblywitch met him and he noticed how tired and out of breath she was. He offered to lend her his bicycle! She thanked him warmly because it was so very kind . . . . . but who ever heard of a witch riding a bicycle! The days passed and it was no laughing matter. "Meow Maroo," Jet said to Bumblywitch as he wound himself around her much thinner legs.

Imagine a witch who couldn't ride her broomstick or wear proper witch's boots and shoes with buckles. She had eaten less, walked more, worked harder and she did feel better.

"Now I shall try again," she told Jet, as she picked up her elastic-sided witch's boots.

"Meow, Meow, Maroo," said Jet watching Bumblywitch putting on her boots without any trouble at all.

Now for her dear, faithful broomstick. Bumblywitch carried him outside carefully; it was a long time since that dreadful day when she had been too heavy. Bumblywitch sat down very gently and said,

"Broomstick, broomstick,
Now I'm ready.
Travel me quick,
Keep me steady."

It was a magical moment; they rose in the air at once. 'I'm not so fat, I'm not so heavy' thought Bumblywitch, 'and indeed I never will be again. Plenty of exercise, not having a second helping and not being too quick to pop a piece of chocolate in my mouth. In future I will only ride my broomstick when it is necessary and walk at other times. It is really very easy if you put your mind to it.'

"Now we will go over to see my sisters," she told the broomstick. "We can tell each other our new spells"

It would be fun to see if they noticed that she was thinner. Last time she had seen them, Grumblywitch and Fumblywitch had cackled a little unkindly and said that her shadow was getting larger.

Whoops, the broomstick dipped and swerved quite alarmingly because Bumblywitch wasn't thinking. "I must pay more attention' she thought, 'after all we are a bit out of practice.'

"Heigho, away we go," said Bumblywitch to the broomstick, and setting a steady course, they sailed over the trees and vanished out of sight.

THE PUMBLECHOKE ROCKET

Mr Pumblechoke was bored. He had cleaned his car, cut the lawn, dug the garden and put up a new shelf in his kitchen. His house was spick and span and his garden neat and tidy. That's why he was bored.

He sighed, and picked up a magazine. On the front cover there was a picture of a spaceship. A shiny, silver spaceship with hundreds of dials and levers and switches. Mr Pumblechoke was very interested in Space. In fact, he had written to the American President three times, asking if he could be an astronaut. But, each time he had received a polite reply, saying that old people were not allowed into Space. They might get dizzy.

After studying the picture for some time, Mr Pumblechoke had a brilliant idea. He decided to copy the picture and build his own spaceship in the back garden. He could go to the Moon all by himself!

In the weeks that followed, he didn't have time to be bored. He hammered and glued and polished and sprayed. Slowly, the shapeless heap of scrap metal began to look like a rocket. He made knobs out of cotton reels, stuck empty baked-bean cans together for the exhaust pipes and nailed a cuckoo clock inside so he could time his journey. He sprayed the whole rocket with silver paint and wrote "The Pumblechoke Lunar Rocket" on one side in red letters. It looked marvellous!

"I'm going to the Moon, Mrs Wobblethorpe!" he called to his neighbour, "I'll bring you back some rock."

Mrs Wobblethorpe went quite pale when she saw the home-made rocket.

"You go careful, Mr Pumblechoke," she said. "You're not getting any younger, you know."

A large flowerpot covered with silver foil and two eye-holes and a mouth cut in it made a super space helmet. Then, Mr Pumblechoke carefully painted his old overalls and boots with silver paint. He packed some food and a map and decided to take off the next morning.

The alarm clock rang at five o'clock and Mr Pumblechoke leapt out of bed. He was so excited. He put on his space outfit and hurried downstairs for breakfast. He had to take off his space helmet, because he couldn't eat his cornflakes with it on. Then he rushed out to check the rocket's engines.

Everything was perfect! He looked up to check that there were no birds or planes flying overhead and pressed the ignition button. The engines fired and the rocket slowly and gracefully lifted into the air. Mr Pumblechoke beamed. "We have lift-off!" he said to himself.

As the rocket gained speed, Mr Pumblechoke watched from the window as the land grew smaller and smaller. He planned to be on the Moon by suppertime and he would have banana sandwiches and chocolate cake to celebrate.

He was just checking his food supply when the rocket suddenly turned to the left and hurtled on into the darkness. Mr Pumblechoke checked his map. This wasn't the way to the Moon. In fact, it was the way to nowhere!

Some hours later, Mr Pumblechoke, who was rather worried by this time, saw a bright light in the distance. He put on the brakes and started to slow down. The bright light became bigger and bigger.

"It must be a planet," he said to himself. He didn't know which one, but he decided to land anyway.

The rocket bumped down gently on the dusty surface.

Mr Pumblechoke opened the door and climbed down the steps. To his surprise, the rocket was surrounded by funny little people. They were very small with pointed noses and chins. They all had green curly hair and wore red spacesuits.

Mr Pumblechoke felt dizzy with shock. "Er, excuse me," he said, "I'm Mr Pumblechoke, Arnold Pumblechoke. Is this the Moon?"

The funny little people laughed, and one replied,

"He wants to know just where the Moon is
Doesn't he know that we're the Loonies?
Only in rhyme can we converse
We call our planet the Looniverse."

Mr Pumblechoke smiled. The Loonies led him to a large building. Inside, there were tables laden with food.

"After your meal, you come with us
A sight-seeing trip in our Looniverse bus," said a Loony.
Another pulled at his sleeve.

"I'm the bus driver. I am clever
Will you stay here forever and ever?'

Mr Pumblechoke explained that he was only taking a short trip, because he was bored at home.

The Loonies all crammed into the Loonibus and Mr Pumblechoke sat at the front. They trundled in and out of Loonicraters, up and down dried up Loonirivers and along dry, dusty Loonitracks until they had seen the whole of the Looniverse. There were also large Loonibeasts that lived in the Loonicaves. Mr Pumblechoke thought it was wonderful.

They all jumped out of the Loonibus and Mr Pumblechoke sat down
quickly on a rock.

"If your head feels rather queer
It is our different atmosphere," said a Loony.

"We all felt like you at first
We thought our heads were going to burst," said another.

Mr Pumblechoke liked the Loonies very much, but he felt it was time he
went home. The Loonies all crowded round him.

"Please say you'll stay and be our King
You will get used to everything," said one.

"No one ever comes to see us here
You are the first for many a year," said another.

Mr Pumblechoke shook his head. "My home is far away," he said. He
thanked them all and shook hands with everyone. Then he climbed the
steps of his rocket.

'Goodbye, everyone and thank you again. I should be home by half past
ten," he said.

The Loonies cheered loudly and
he realised he had spoken in rhyme.

The rocket door closed behind him
and the engines burst into life once
more. He waved until the Loonies
were out of sight and set the engines
at full speed for home.

The hours soon passed by and the cuckoo in the clock came out ten times. Mr Pumblechoke looked out of the window and could see land clearly, like a twinkling fairyland below him. He carefully steered the rocket down right over his back garden.

He crashed into a big leafy tree but luckily was not hurt. He felt very silly hanging from a branch by his trousers. He wriggled himself free and started to walk home. The silver foil was peeling from his helmet and the silver paint was flaking from his spacesuit. He was very glad everyone was in bed.

He arrived home, tired but happy. He opened the kitchen door and found Mrs Wobblethorpe waiting for him with a nice, hot drink.

"Welcome home," she said. Mr Pumblechoke sipped his drink.

"Next time I'm bored," he said, "I'll play a game of cards. That doesn't make me dizzy!"

GOLD

There's gold in the meadows
And gold in the trees;
It shines on the buttercups,
It shimmers on leaves.
There are golden-eyed daisies
And marigolds to pluck;
Bright gold of the daffodils
Pale gold of the duck.

There's gold on the eagle
And small crested bird;
There are fine golden fishes
In thousands, I've heard.
There's gold that men dig for
Down in the earth;
Then bury in Banks
And count up its worth.

But listen, Great Sun,
As you sink in the west:
Your gold so warm
Is the loveliest.

THE MAGIC COMBS

"King Bonkers may be my father," said Princess Mirabelle, as she brushed the mud from the coat of her little dog, "but I think he must be the silliest King that ever lived."

"King Bonkers may be my husband," said the Queen as she pruned her favourite rose bush, "but I have to agree with you. If he isn't complaining how bored he is, he is playing silly tricks on people. Everybody is tired of him and if he doesn't mend his ways soon, the people will choose a new King and we shall all be turned out of our beautiful palace."

King Bonkers walked across the lawn towards the Queen and Princess.

"I am so bored," he said.

"We could all be bored if we walked around all day doing nothing," said the Queen. "Have you signed your important papers today?"

"No," answered King Bonkers. "Important papers bore me."

"Well, you could help me prune the roses," suggested the Queen.

"No thank you," said King Bonkers, "I might prick my fingers." And he walked out of the palace gate and up the hill to Wizard Winegum's house.

Wizard Winegum wasn't very pleased to see King Bonkers.

"Tell me what you want quickly," he said. "I am very busy today."

"I am bored," said King Bonkers, "and I want a spell to make something exciting happen."

Wizard Winegum stroked his long white beard thoughtfully.

"Well hm, well hm, I have some magic combs," he said. "If you comb your hair with one of these combs, everything you touch for half an hour afterwards will turn into something different."

"Into what?" asked King Bonkers.

"That's the trouble," answered Wizard Winegum. "You won't know until you touch it. The combs are quite expensive. Twenty gold pieces each."

"I will take two," said King Bonkers and he counted out forty gold pieces.

"Are you quite sure you want two?" asked Wizard Winegum, taking the combs down from his high shelf. "Surely one will be enough?"

"I want two," said King Bonkers and he took the combs and ran back to the palace as fast as his little fat legs would carry him.

Puffing and panting he ran up the stairs to the Queen's bedroom. The Queen was sitting at her dressing table brushing her hair.

"I have bought you a nice new comb, dear," said King Bonkers handing her one of the combs.

"Oh thank you, that is kind of you," she said and she combed her hair with the magic comb. She then put the comb down and picked up her hair brush.

As soon as she touched it, the brush turned into a spider. The Queen hated spiders. She screamed and dropped the spider. It fell onto her lap.

She tried to knock the spider from her lap onto the floor but as she touched it, it turned into a mouse. The Queen was terrified of mice. She climbed onto a chair screaming to King Bonkers to take the mouse away.

As she touched the chair it turned into a kangaroo. It hopped out of the door with the Queen clinging to its neck.

King Bonkers thought this was very funny and laughed and laughed until the tears ran down his fat cheeks.

Still laughing, King Bonkers went to give the other comb to Princess Mirabelle. The princess was playing with her little dog on her bedroom floor. King Bonkers handed her the comb.

"Oh thank you, father," she said, and combed her hair with the new comb.

She picked up a slide to put in her hair. At once the slide turned into a ginger kitten. The ginger kitten scratched her and wriggled out of her hands. It ran through the bedroom door and down the stairs chased by the princess's little dog.

Princess Mirabelle ran to the door to call her dog back. As she touched the door it turned into a horse. The horse ran down the stairs after the dog and the kitten.

Soon the whole palace was in an uproar with the kangaroo, dog, horse, kitten and mouse all chasing each other.

King Bonkers hadn't had so much fun for years. He laughed and laughed until he thought his sides would burst.

The next morning, King Bonkers left the palace bright and early to buy two more magic combs from Wizard Winegum.

Princess Mirabelle watched him from her bedroom window. She felt sure he was up to no good and had something to do with what had happened the day before. She decided to follow him.

She crouched down outside Wizard Winegum's door and listened through the keyhole as King Bonkers told the Wizard how pleased he had been with the combs and that he wanted to buy two more.

Princess Mirabelle ran back to the palace and told the Queen all she had overheard.

The Queen was very angry. "King Bonkers needs to be taught a lesson he will not forget in a hurry," she said. She bent down and whispered something in Princess Mirabelle's ear.

Princess Mirabelle smiled as she and the Queen went into the bedroom. They both sat down in front of the Queen's dressing table and started to brush their hair.

King Bonkers was very pleased to see them together when he entered the bedroom. It would save him a walk. He gave them a comb each and sat down on the Queen's bed to wait for the fun to begin.

After thanking him politely, the Queen and the Princess combed their hair with the magic combs AND THEN stood up together and walked slowly over to King Bonkers. The Queen put out her hand and touched King Bonkers on the top of his bald head.

King Bonkers turned into a big, fat round ball.

"Oh look!" said the Queen to Princess Mirabelle. "What a pretty ball. Throw it out of the window and see how well it bounces."

"Oh NO NO NO. I'm not a ball I'm ME!" shouted King Bonkers, but the Queen and the Princess pretended not to hear him.

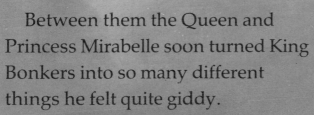

Princess Mirabelle picked up the ball and at once the King turned into a frog.

"What a horrid frog," said the Queen. "Give it to me and I will put it in the fish pond."

"No, no. I'm not a frog, please don't put me in the fish pond. I can't swim," pleaded the King.

Between them the Queen and Princess Mirabelle soon turned King Bonkers into so many different things he felt quite giddy.

At last he turned into a little bird and flew out of the window and hid himself in a large oak tree.

"Oh dear, oh dear," he said. "I am so dizzy with all this changing. I haven't enjoyed it at all. I will never again use magic to play silly tricks on people." As he spoke, King Bonkers turned back into a King once more. He was a very fat king so it took him a long time to climb down from the tree.

"Oh dear, oh dear," he thought. "I do hope nobody sees me. It is so undignified for a *King* to have to climb down from a tree."

On reaching the ground he looked carefully around but fortunately no one was in sight. Full of his new resolve, he quickly returned to the palace and it wasn't long before he was renowned for his wisdom and good sense.

NED OF THE TODDIN'S GAME

Ned of the Toddin was a very unusual kitten, with pointed ears and a twitchy tail. One day, he decided to go for a walk in the orchard which stood near his home. There stood rows of apple trees with their shiny red apples hanging from them like presents from a Christmas tree. The wind was blowing a little, and all the leaves made a swishing noise as they swayed to and fro. SWISH. SWAY. SWISH. SWISH. SWAY. SWISH. Just like that.

Suddenly, as Ned was walking underneath the trees, one of the apples fell down and hit him on his furry head. He was very surprised indeed, and he sat down and looked carefully at the apple. Then he patted it with his furry paw, as any cat might have done when he was not sure what to do next. Then he looked at the tree crossly.

"If you do that again," he said, "I'll shake all your apples down with my twitchy tail."

The apple tree was much too busy swishing in the wind to listen, and sure enough another apple fell to the ground. THUMP. Just like that. Ned of the Toddin became very cross indeed. His twitchy tail twitched, and his little claws came out. He ran up to the tree, and caught hold of the rough trunk with his twitchy tail. He shook and shook until all the apples had fallen to the ground in a heap. There were so many of them that you couldn't see the grass at all, only the shiny red apples. When the farmer came along, he was very surprised indeed to see so many apples had fallen down at once.

"Well, I don't know," he said.

In the meantime, Ned went on his way. He hadn't gone far when he came upon a field where corn had been cut by a machine and tied up into big square bundles. He decided to have a quiet cat-nap in the gentle warm sunshine, so he lay down in the field and blinked sleepily, for all the world like the sort of kitten who sleeps all day because he is too lazy to do anything else.

He hadn't been lying there long when he heard a small pattering noise. PATTER. PATTER. PATTER. Just like that. The noise got nearer, and nearer, until it was just behind one of the square bundles. Then a pair of floppy ears appeared, then two brown eyes, then a nose and then a whole rabbit sprang happily over the bundle. His name was Burrowdeep Carroteater.

"Hallo little kitten," he said. "Would you like to play?"

Ned of the Toddin jumped up straight away, and he and Burrowdeep Carroteater began to chase each other round the square bundle of corn.

"Boo!" said Burrowdeep Carroteater.

"Mew!" said Ned.

"Boo!"

"Mew!"

They began to run merrily about all over the field.

Now, because they were playing, they didn't notice that a red fox with a bushy tail had crept right up behind them. He had little white teeth, and wicked little eyes that shone like hot sparks. No one was cleverer than he. His name was Reynold Redbrush, and he was the most dreaded fox in all the neighbourhood. Suddenly, he jumped out in front of poor Burrowdeep and glared at him very fiercely indeed.

"Come here, master rabbit," he said. "My children are hungry, and they want you for their supper."

"Help!" said Burrowdeep Carroteater. "What shall I do?"

Just then, Ned of the Toddin came and sat on the grass beside him. If you didn't notice the faint gleam in his eyes you would have thought he was the most harmless kitten in the world.

"Go away, little kitten," said Reynold Redbrush. "My children don't want you for their supper."

"You must go away yourself," said Ned, "or I'll pull off your bushy tail with my sharp claws."

67

Now Reynold Redbrush was not a very patient fox, and you could see that he was getting rather annoyed. His little white teeth ground together, and his wicked little eyes sparkled more than ever.

"Ow! Ow!" he barked. "My children can eat a kitten for their supper just as well as a rabbit."

He began to creep forward very slowly, as if he wasn't *really* doing anything of the sort. In the meantime, Burrowdeep Carroteater made his escape. He leaped up and ran across the field for all he was worth, until all you could see of him was his little white tail.

Ned of the Toddin sat very still, for all the world as if he hadn't noticed the crafty fox at all. Then, in a flash, he jumped up and ran over to where two square bundles of corn had been stacked together to make a little den. Reynold Redbrush ran after him, and chased him all round the corn den, sometimes under it, sometimes over it. But Ned was always a bit too far in front, because he could run very fast indeed.

"Come and be eaten, little kitten," cried Reynold Redbrush.

"Come and catch me," said nimble Ned.

Then Reynold Redbrush had a crafty idea. He decided to wait inside the little corn den, and catch Ned as he came round the corner. But this was exactly what Ned wanted him to do. As quick as lightning, Ned caught hold of the square bundles of corn with his twitchy tail. He pulled hard. PUUUUULL. Just like that. The corn den came toppling down on Reynold Redbrush and squashed him flat. All you could see was the tip of his black nose, the tip of his bushy tail, and the tip of his four paws.

"Ow," he said, feeling very sorry for himself.

Ned of the Toddin jumped up on top of the square bundle of corn, and curled up in the warm sunshine ready to go to sleep. Before he went to sleep, he sang himself a little cat's cradle song, as all kittens sometimes do. "Prrrrrr," it went. "Prrrrrr."

SING-LO AND THE DRAGON

Long ago, in a small village in China there was great excitement. A messenger from the great Emperor in Peking had called all the people into the village square, because he had something very important to tell them. They knew he came from the Emperor because he was dressed in fine silken robes and wore a hat with golden tassels. The two soldiers who stood beside him, blew a fanfare on their long curved horns when everyone was assembled. The crowd was silent as the old man was handed a scroll made of parchment. In a loud voice he began to read:

"The Emperor wishes it to be known that the Royal Dragon has escaped. There will be a big reward for anyone who can find him and an even bigger reward for anyone who is able to capture and return the Dragon to the Royal Palace."

When he had finished reading, he handed the scroll to one of his attendants who hung it up for everyone to see.

As the messenger left the village to spread the news, there was much talk among the people. It was well known that the Emperor kept a fierce, red dragon near the Palace gates to guard his many treasures. The thought of a fierce Dragon roaming about the streets frightened the people. They fled to their homes and locked the doors and windows.

At the end of the village, there lived an old woman with her grandson, Sing-Lo. She was old and did not go out into the village very often. Sing-Lo stopped on his way home from school so that he could listen to the Emperor's messenger and tell his grandmother. He heard the announcement with surprise; who would be able to catch a fire-breathing dragon or even get anywhere near one? Sing-Lo hurried home to practise flying his kite before supper, as there was going to be a prize given at school at the end of the week for the boy who could fly his kite the highest.

Soon he set off up the hill overlooking his home, singing merrily. He had quite forgotten all about the fierce red dragon as he climbed higher and higher in search of a good place for flying his kite.

Suddenly he became aware of being quite alone. He looked back down onto the village and there too, the streets were quiet and empty. Only then did he remember the words of the old man from the Emperor's Palace. He went on anyway, he couldn't see any Dragons about.

The evening was very warm and Sing-Lo sat down for a short rest. There were many caves nearby but Sing-Lo had never been inside them. A strange feeling came over him. He could sense he was not alone – someone was watching him. Turning round he could see two very large eyes looking at him from the darkness of one of the caves.

Sing-Lo nearly jumped out of his skin. Could this be the dragon, he wondered? "Who's there?" he whispered.

A gentle snort came from inside the cave and a deep voice said, "Don't be afraid. I am Kwang Fu, the Dragon and I've escaped from the Emperor's Palace. I'm tired of breathing fire all day and scaring everyone. I really want to be a friendly Dragon but no one will come anywhere near me."

"Oh!" cried Sing-Lo, feeling much happier. "May I be your friend? I don't know anything about dragons but I'm willing to learn."

72

Kwang Fu was so pleased he had found a friend to talk to that he forgot to breathe fire and came slowly out of the cave. He was so big that Sing-Lo took a few steps backwards.

"I ran away because I like it up here. I feel as free as the wind and I shall never, never return to the Palace. The only thing is – I do feel so very hungry. Have you anything in your pockets to eat?" said the Dragon.

"Sorry," said Sing-Lo, "but I can bring you something tomorrow. What would you like?"

"Big juicy oranges," snorted Kwang Fu. "I get so dry breathing fire. Oranges are the fruit I like best." He wagged his tail from side to side, knocking a couple of trees completely over as he did so.

Sing-Lo said, "Leave it to me," but he really didn't know how he was going to find enough oranges to feed a hungry dragon. He knew he would have to try. Then he remembered his friend who had a fruit stall in the market. Surely his friend would let him have some oranges at the end of the day.

73

Every evening that week, Sing-Lo went up the hillside to the cave with as many oranges as he could carry. He thought it best to say nothing to anyone about the Dragon, as Kwang Fu was determined to stay in the cave, but it would only be a matter of time before the Emperor's soldiers found him and took him back to the Palace.

"You can't stop here forever," said Sing-Lo on his next visit.

"I can, I can," said the Dragon. "As long as you bring me oranges," he added under his breath.

"What will you do when winter comes?" asked his friend, thinking he had caught him out.

"I can easily breathe fire and warm up the cave," said Kwang Fu.

Sing-Lo knew that he could not keep on coming to feed the dragon. His grandmother was beginning to ask questions about where he was going every evening. So he decided to go and see the Emperor's minister who was very pleased to have news of the dragon, at last. The Emperor had become very bad-tempered since Kwang Fu had escaped. You see, he was the only ruler who had his own red dragon to guard his treasures.

"Whatever can we do?" asked Sing-Lo.

"Well, now," said the minister, stroking his long white beard. "It seems to me that Kwang Fu is very lonely."

"Yes, yes," said Sing-Lo. "Perhaps you could ask the Emperor to find another dragon to keep him company, because he does need a friend."

75

The minister told the Emperor, who agreed, and very soon a young dragon was found and placed in the Palace grounds. Sing-Lo went to the cave to tell Kwang Fu.

"I shall NEVER, NEVER come down!" he stamped.

"Well, if you don't come down, no one will ever like you and you will never have another friend," said Sing-Lo. "Good-bye, Kwang Fu, I can't help you any more." He went away feeling very sad, because he had tried so hard to help his friend.

Kwang Fu felt very sad too, when Sing-Lo had gone. It would be nice to have a friend, and after all, it was lonely in the cave.

The next night, Kwang Fu crept back into the Palace grounds. Everyone was pleased to see him once more at the Royal Gates. The Emperor was smiling again and Sing-Lo was summoned to the Palace.

"I give you my word that there will always be plenty of oranges for the dragons," said the Emperor. "I feel sure they will soon become great friends. You are a very brave little fellow and I have a reward for you."

Sing-Lo and his grandmother were overjoyed at their rich reward and when he grew up, the Emperor made Sing-Lo Chief Keeper of Dragons at the Palace.

77

MY CLOWN

As I was walking in the town,
I met a pale-faced, painted clown;
"Good-day!" said he, "Good-day!" said I;
He tossed his hat and winked an eye.

"I hope you'll come to see the show,
You'll love the animals, I know.
One man he walks the wire up top;
The folks all gasp – for fear he'll drop.

Then pretty girls swing – swift and neat;
They even hang on by their feet!
And four young boys in dazzling jeans
Turn somersaults on trampolines."

"I'm sorry, sir," I had to say,
"I cannot come – I cannot pay."
"Why, that's too bad," my clown then said,
"Look, here's a pass for you instead."

I washed my face, I combed my hair,
I started early – I was there!
I handed in the pass and so,
Was taken to the first front row.

Prancing horses, gaily plumed,
Coats agleaming – so well groomed;
A crowd of clowns – I counted six!
All tumbling down and playing tricks.

The lights, the costumes – they were grand
And music from the big brass band;
Elephants huge and ponies small
It would take a week to tell you all.

I'll not forget that circus night,
Or my kind clown, pale-faced and white;
If we should meet, I'll call out, "Hi!"
And watch him wink his painted eye.

79

GRUMBLYWITCH

Cherry Blossom Cottage was indeed a pretty place. There were roses growing round the door, the garden was neat and tidy and so was the cottage itself. Grumblywitch and her cat lived there. The cat's name was Odd because he had one green eye and one yellow one, which is not unusual when you belong to a witch! Poor Grumblywitch made life very hard for herself. She was never satisfied, nothing was ever good enough unless it was perfect. Everything had to be tidy in the cottage and the garden because she was so fussy.

Just now, she was over at Ritchie Willy the Cobbler's house, moving a swarm of bees from his newly-painted front door. The bees liked the yellow paint on Ritchie Willy's door much better than the tree trunk which was their home. Ritchie Willy wanted them to go away.

"Come bees, come away I say
   Buzzing, buzzing, come this way,"
commanded Grumblywitch.
The humming mass of bees on the
door parted to let the Queen Bee out.
She rose in the air and landed on the
top of the tall hat worn by
Grumblywitch. At the same time, all
the rest of the bees followed and
settled on her.

   "Are you alright?" asked Ritchie
Willy, because the witch's hat was a
solid mass of buzzing bees.

Grumblywitch did not answer
him. Getting on to her broomstick,
she rose straight up into the air and
whirled away over the trees. This
took the bees by surprise. They fell
off her hat but still followed her, like
a wisp of black smoke.

"Come with me, into my hive,
 If you wish to stay alive,"
said Grumblywitch crossly to the
bees as she landed in her garden.
The Queen Bee was still sitting on
her hat, indeed, everything had
happened so quickly that the poor
thing did not know where she was.

Grumblywitch walked over to an
empty beehive by her potato patch
and spoke to the Queen and the
bees.

"Settle down and honey make
 No more journeys will you take."
Quickly the bees swarmed and with
their Queen, buzzed into the
beehive.

Grumblywitch felt that she had
been a little cross with Ritchie Willy.
She had not even said goodbye to
him. Oh dear, she was getting so
grumpy and cross lately. As she
went into her cottage, Odd the cat,
ran out to her and wound his tail
round her legs.

"Mind what you do, cat," cried
Grumblywitch. "My feet hurt, I am
tired and I want to sit down." She
had forgotten her breakfast that
morning and her stomach rumbled
and grumbled, as she was beginning
to feel very hungry. The cat said
rather cheekily.

"Witch Grumbly? Grumblywitch?
Witch Rumbly! Rumblywitch!"

"Odd is right, I *am* 'grumblyrumbly' and oh, how my poor feet hurt," said Grumblywitch as she put on the kettle to make some tea. This, and taking off her boots made her feel better. Her feet were her problem and that is a terrible thing for a witch. Her witch's boots pinched her feet, but she could not go out of her cottage without them. She had to wear them when she had work to do, no matter how much they hurt.

Grumblywitch gave the cat a saucer of milk and stroked him gently. Grumblywitch might be her name but she was not grumpy really, it was just that her feet made her cross. She filled a bowl with warm water, poured herself a cup of tea and put the bowl on the floor. She put her aching feet down into the warm water.

Just then, Ritchie Willy walked in through the door. When Grumblywitch came home feeling tired and cross, she had not closed it properly. Odd the cat, ran to greet him because they were very good friends and he was pleased to see him.

Grumblywitch was not so pleased. How terrible that Ritchie Willy should see her soaking her feet. If she had not been in such a hurry to get her boots off, she would not have forgotten to close the door.

"Grit and gravel," she said crossly to herself. She would have to stay where she was, she could not do anything else.

"You moved those bees, it was so kind. Your door was open . . . I hope you do not mind." Ritchie Willy stopped speaking as he saw Grumblywitch glaring at him. Indeed, he was greatly concerned because being a cobbler, the boots and shoes that people wore were his trade. Oh dear me, he thought as he saw her poor swollen feet. Now he knew why the witch had been off in such a hurry.

"Dear witch," he said. "It was so good of you to rid me of those tiresome bees. You left my garden before I had time to ask what I could do for you in return. You are always doing things for me."

Feeling so ashamed of herself, Grumblywitch felt a 'humblywitch'. How could she have been so cross with such a nice old man?

"How good of you to come," she said. "I am sorry I went off like that. It is no use pretending, Ritchie Willy, my feet are very sore. What can I do?"

Ritchie Willy knew exactly how he could repay her kindness. He could see that her boots were much too small. It was easy to help her, he would make her a new pair of boots.

"Please will you let me make you a new pair of boots, just like these, but in a size which will be more comfortable?" he asked.

Both Grumblywitch and the cat
were very pleased. Happy days
would be here again for them if her
feet were better. So she accepted and
when she had dried her feet, Ritchie
Willy measured them carefully and,
bidding her goodbye, went back to
his cottage.

Ritchie Willy worked all through the night and early the next morning,
he left the boots outside the cottage door.

When Grumblywitch opened the door to let Odd out, she found a lovely new pair of soft, black, elastic-sided boots. She tried them on at once. They were perfect. They were so comfortable that she did a little hop, skip and a jump.

Her stomach made its usual rumbly noise, reminding her that neither she nor the cat had eaten any breakfast yet. She made some tea and gave Odd some milk. This time she made herself hot buttered toast and enjoyed it. Then she and Odd sat in front of the fire feeling very happy and contented.

"I'll go and see my sisters, that is what I will do,

Riding my broomstick . . . and I'll take you,"

Grumblywitch told Odd. That was a good idea, for it was many moons since she had seen Bumblywitch and Fumblywitch. They might notice her lovely new boots and as she did not feel cross anymore they might notice that too!

So Grumblywitch and her cat Odd, flew away on her broomstick over the trees.

FREDDY FROG

A little frog upon a leaf
Went sailing down the river,
His friends all playing on the bank
Saw Freddy shake and shiver.

He knew the river's water fast
Would take him to the sea;
"Jump, jump!" they cried, "You silly frog!
It's easy as can be."

"I can't, I can't!" he cried in fear
"I'm scared and I'm not clever."
"You must, you must!" they called again
"Make haste! It's now or never!"

A handsome swan, quite fond of frogs
Came gliding close to catch him;
"A tasty morsel, I declare!"
And stretched his neck to snatch him.

Then Freddy knew he had to jump
"I will not be his dinner!"
He flung himself into the air –
His leap, it was a winner!

"I can, I can!" he laughed with glee
And swam and swam delighted,
Back to his friends upon the bank
All dancing and excited.

THE BIRTHDAY PRESENT

There was once a good and wise King who ruled over a kingdom where the streams were full of fish, the trees full of birds and the houses full of happy people. King Casper was such a good king that his subjects wanted to give him a very special birthday present. So the Prime Minister went to visit the Fairy Queen. She agreed that Casper was a good king. She had a wonderful present for the people to give him. It was a short, red velvet cloak, with tiny silver tassels.

When the Prime Minister returned, the people were disappointed with it.

"Wait!" said the Prime Minister. "The King can keep this cloak for one week only." The people were even more dismayed. "But here's the secret," he went on. "During that time, anyone who wears the cloak will receive a magic gift."

All the people clapped and cheered and the Prime Minister set off to present the cloak to King Casper.

The King was delighted. He wore the cloak to his birthday party and was very proud of it.

"Let's have some music," he called, for King Casper loved music.

"Well," replied his daughter Miranda. "If you want music, why don't you sing and play for us?"

King Casper laughed until his sides ached. It was an old family joke that he could play the piano with one finger only and had a voice like a rusty hinge.

Thinking it was a birthday trick, King Casper sat down at the piano. His hands began to move across the keys as if they had always done so. He was amazed to find himself not only playing but singing a merry tune. Then Miranda told him about the magic cloak and that now he would always be able to play beautiful music. King Casper was very happy.

In a little while, he decided that he would go down to the palace kitchens where the cook was preparing his birthday meal. The King was far too kind to say so, but his cook was certainly not the best cook in the land. Often the meals were burnt and tasteless, but King Casper never complained.

While he was inspecting the kitchens, the King said,

"How cold it is down here, you have no windows to let in the sunshine. You must wear my cloak this afternoon to keep you warm."

The cook knelt before the King in thanks. Everything the cook made that day and from then on, was delicious. King Casper had the finest birthday feast he had ever had and the cook was delighted.

After the party, King Casper rubbed his hands in glee.

"I must make good use of this magic cloak," he said. "I shall go and visit some of my ministers."

This took two days, as the King and his ministers spent hours talking about the affairs of the kingdom. The King quite forgot the magic cloak.

When he arrived back at the palace, the cloak was missing. King Casper felt too ashamed to tell anyone. He simply could not remember where he had left it.

Next day, the sun was so warm that he took his family to spend the day at the lake where it was cool. All day, he thought and thought, but still he could not remember where he had left his cloak.

On the following day, he rode round his kingdom. It looked so beautiful as the sun shone on the trees, the lawns and the silver streams. But he was troubled at heart. Where had he left the cloak?

By the next evening, King Casper was very worried. The cloak was his for only one more day, then it would return to fairyland. He had wasted so much time. He sat on his balcony watching a beautiful sunset.

Suddenly he knew. The sun! It had been shining for three days. There could be no doubt, he had left the cloak with the Minister of Weather. Of course, the King was right. He collected the cloak at once.

Now the King knew that his daughter had always wanted to have long hair but she just could not make it grow. It scarcely altered day by day.

So the King took the cloak and tiptoed into Miranda's bedroom. She was fast asleep. Taking care not to wake her, King Casper spread the cloak over her. Early in the morning, he went again to her room. The magic cloak had disappeared.

When Miranda woke, as she leapt out of bed, her hair fell around her shoulders in long, golden ringlets. Throwing her arms around the King, she cried happily,

"Father, look at my hair! It must have been the magic cloak."

So there had to be another celebration. The Princess wore her prettiest dress and good King Casper made up a new song. As they sang and danced on the palace balcony, the people in the market place below began dancing too. It was such a happy sight and the warm sun shone on them all.

TAB'S WISH

Mother cat looked at her little kitten and said, "One day you will be a fine looking cat with lovely green eyes and a grey back with black stripes. I shall call you Tab, because I can see that you will be a clever tabby cat."

Tab lived with her mother at Buttercup Farm. Each day she grew bigger and bigger until she was a grownup cat. Her body was not too fat but it was strong. In the daytime she could kill a rat with one stroke of her paw, and she didn't need to open her eyes wide to do that, but when Tab went out at night to hunt rabbits she opened her eyes wide until they were big and round. She was such a clever cat, she caught more rats on the farm than the white cat; she caught more rats than the black cat and even more rats than the ginger tomcat. In fact, she was the cleverest cat on the farm.

Tab had a secret which she told to no one, not even her mother . . . she wanted to fly . . . that would be more exciting than catching rats. The cheeky little birds who teased her would not get away from her so easily if she could fly.

Tab tried many times to fly. She climbed on high walls, she climbed into trees, but when she jumped, she never went up – up – up – , she went down – down – down and always landed with her feet on the ground. She did not fly, no matter how many times she tried.

One morning, Tab left the farm to find out how to fly, and down the lane she went until she reached a large field where there was a circus. In the middle of the field was a big red and white tent from the top of which a flag was flying. At one side of the field there were caravans belonging to the circus people and on the other side there were animal cages and more tents. Little children who came to this circus always came to see the animals after the show.

Tab had never seen a circus before, so she stopped and listened. She heard people talking, horses neighing and dogs barking. Then she looked at the poster on the gate. It was a picture of a man inside a red and white tent. He was flying through the air from a trapeze. Tab saw a tent in the middle of the field and so she went through the gate to find him. She crept into the tent and sat beside the circus ring and what did she see?

She saw clowns tumbling over each other. She saw a man standing upside-down on another man's head. She saw a lady riding a cycle which only had one wheel and no handlebars at all. Then she looked up and there he was – the man in the picture – right at the top of the tent. She watched him fly from one trapeze to another, over and over again. Everyone was getting ready for the show.

When the man from the trapeze came down the rope ladder to the ground, Tab ran to ask him how to fly, but one of the clowns saw her. He picked up a broom and chased her out of the tent.

''Shoo! Shoo! Be off with you,'' he cried, and Tab ran quickly across the field to the animal cages, to ask the animals if they knew how to fly.

First she went to the monkeys and said, "My name is Tab. I can run and jump and climb, but I want to fly. Can you please tell me how to fly?"

The big monkey stopped eating his banana and said, "We can run and jump and climb. We can curl our tails round the swing to hang upside-down, but we cannot tell you how to fly. Ask the elephants to help you."

A big elephant held up his trunk in the air . . . he could smell Tab coming nearer and nearer. Tab walked over to him, very, very slowly, for the elephant was so big and Tab was so small.

"Who are you . . . and what do you want?" asked the elephant as he swung his trunk from side to side.

"My name is Tab," she said. "I can run and jump and climb, but I want to fly. Can you please tell me how to fly?"

"I can run too," replied the elephant. "Even though I'm so big, I can balance on my two front legs on the top of a small tub. I can curl up my trunk to put food in my mouth. I use the end of it to pick up a small lump of sugar, but I cannot fly. Perhaps the sea lion can help you . . . he's in the next tent."

Tab went into the tent and sat beside a big tank full of water, but when some of it splashed over the top, she quickly climbed up a ladder and sat on the top step to speak to the sea lion.

"My name is Tab," she said. "I can run and jump and climb but I want to fly. Can you please tell me how to fly?"

The sea lion looked up at Tab and said, "I cannot run but I can swim. I'm clever at catching fish thrown to me. I can climb up that ladder with a ball balanced on my nose, but I cannot tell you how to fly."

Tab asked all the animals how to fly, but the lions could not help her, the tigers could not help her and the horses could not help her, not one of the animals could help her; so poor Tab left the field feeling very tired. She went down the lane and into the park. She sat beside a seat to watch the children's kites and balloons flying in the sky. She wished that she was flying up there too.

Soon two little girls came to sit on the seat and one of them said, "There's a field at the other end of the village where you can fly up in the sky in a balloon."

"I know," replied the other. "It's part of the circus."

This was just what Tab wanted to hear. She set off at once to find the field, but was very tired when she reached it. She didn't see any balloons up in the sky, but on the ground there was a big basket with a lot of ropes tied to it.

Tab walked all round the basket. Then she leaped into it and found it so comfortable that she curled up and fell fast asleep. She was soon awakened by the sound of people shouting.

"Hurrah! Hurrah! It's going up!"

Tab looked over the side of the basket. She was ready to jump out, but the ground was too far away and the people looked very small. She looked up and saw that all the ropes were now fastened to a big balloon, and the two men who were in the basket with her didn't seem to mind her being there at all.

Tab's wish had come true . . . she was flying . . . not like the birds, not like the man in the circus, but in an air balloon. The balloon glided slowly across the sky. As they passed over the village and over the park, they flew right over the circus and Tab wondered if the man on the trapeze was watching.

All went well until black clouds passed over the balloon and the wind began to blow. The balloon went up and then down, up and down, up and down as the wind whistled all around, and Tab began to feel quite sick. Then the basket began to sway from side to side. When Tab looked down again, the fields were going round and round, and the circus was going round and round. In fact, everything below was going round and round, and Tab was now quite giddy. She did not like this part of flying at all and wished that she was back on the ground.

She curled up in the bottom of the basket and there she stayed until she heard people shouting again.

"It's coming down! It's coming down!" they cried.

As soon as the basket touched the ground, Tab jumped out. She walked slowly out of the field through the park, down the lane, past the circus and back to Buttercup Farm.

Tab's secret wish had come true . . . she had wanted to fly . . . she had tried it, but she never wanted to do it again. It was much more fun chasing rats and rabbits, but she never tired of telling all the animals on the farm about her adventures in a hot-air balloon.

DESMOND THE DRAGON

It was a beautiful morning. A pale wintry sun was just rising over the hills. King Gustav decided that he could not stay in bed a moment longer. For once, he would be up before the servants and take a walk in his lovely Castle grounds.

The King struggled with the great iron bars on the Castle door. It would be so good to breathe the fresh morning air. He pulled the doors wide . . . and gave a cry of terror! The beautiful morning was spoilt for there, sitting on his very doorstep, was Desmond the Dragon.

King Gustav was a brave man and a good man. His kingdom was a happy contented place. There was only one thing that spoilt life for King Gustav and his subjects . . . Desmond the Dragon. Desmond the Dragon was the terror of Gustavia. He would storm through the growing wheat fields flattening all before him. Sometimes at night, he breathed flashing fire which burned barns, farmhouses and cottages. No one was safe and no one knew when he would strike.

Now, on this fine sunny morning, the dragon was sitting boldly on the Castle steps. Swiftly, King Gustav reached up to ring the giant alarm bell on the wall. To his amazement, before he could touch it, Desmond, the Dragon sank slowly to his knees. He began to make strange whining sounds, and King Gustav turned to stare at him as he had never heard Desmond do this before.

It was then that King Gustav noticed the baby dragon. It was crouched, shivering beside Desmond, almost hidden behind the enormous creature. The sight of the tiny dragon startled the King and he wondered why Desmond was on his knees making such a pitiful noise.

King Gustav took his hand down from the bell and turned to face his old enemy.

Desmond spoke, "Have mercy, have mercy, good King Gustav. I have come to offer myself to work in your service, if you will save the life of my baby son."

King Gustav could hardly believe his ears. Was this really the fiercest of dragons begging for mercy? Was this some trick? Did the Dragon mean to set fire to his castle as soon as his back was turned? King Gustav was not sure. At that moment, the baby dragon crept right up to the hem of his robe, curled itself up on the warm velvet and fell asleep.

King Gustav was touched as he looked down at the little, sleeping creature. He looked up at Desmond and waited for him to explain.

"His mother died two days ago," said Desmond. "I cannot bring up a baby by myself. If you will care for my son, here in the Castle, I will change my ways and become a good dragon."

King Gustav was a very kind man. He felt he just could not refuse. It would not be easy, but they would look after the baby and Desmond would have his chance.

From that day onwards the King led the Dragon round the Castle grounds on a pair of reins, just like a lead. "Sit!" he would command, and Desmond would flop down in a great heap. "Wait!" he would say, and the Dragon stayed still for hours. Later, let off his lead, Desmond learnt to 'Fetch,' 'Drop,' and 'Beg.' The huge creature would trot everywhere at King Gustav's heels for all the world like a tame hound dog. He slept each night in one of the barns.

Meanwhile, the servants in the Royal nursery had named the baby dragon, Benjamin. They taught him to be good and polite, and so it was that before long, the two dragons almost became part of the family.

Of course, Benjamin was now growing fast. One day, King Gustav decided that Desmond should visit his son at bedtime each evening. The Queen would read a bedtime story to both dragons sitting by the great fire in the Castle hall.

When Benjamin was led off to bed, Desmond would return to sleep in the barn. King Gustav began to notice how Desmond always turned to look with sad, longing eyes at the flames flickering in the fire.

King Gustav knew why the fire made Desmond unhappy. A Dragon is proud because he is able to breathe fire. Since coming to live in the Castle, Desmond had really changed his ways. There was no doubt about it, thought the King, dragons do have a right to be fierce and Desmond had learnt his lessons well. He deserved some reward. . . .

So, one evening, after the stories were read, King Gustav did not send Desmond back to the barn.

"I have an important job for you, Desmond," said the King. "You have become a very responsible Dragon. I am going to make you Keeper of the King's Candles."

Desmond looked as if he could not believe his ears. Candles had bright, flickering flames, the flames he loved. Whatever did the King want him to do? King Gustav explained, "Each night about this time, every candle in the castle has to be lit . . . every single one . . . from the largest in the hall to the smallest on the cellar stairs. Whenever we have parties, many more candles will be needed. It's just the job for you, Desmond. You can light each candle with a flash of fire and I shall be pleased for you to do it."

Desmond was delighted. He could be a real dragon again, and when Benjamin grew older, he could help him. Together they would be Keepers of the King's Candles for ever and ever. He leapt into the air with a great roar, crying out, "I must be the luckiest dragon alive."

"Sit!" King Gustav called out with a smile. At once the huge creature was there by his side. "Yes, you are a lucky dragon, and such a well behaved one too," the King told him, patting his scaly head fondly.

Desmond the Dragon turned bright pink with pride.

THE SECRET CAVE

The little train puffed into the station and out tumbled all the excited children, ready for their day near the sea. Bobby was the last to step onto the platform and he wandered along to look at the engine. He loved trains and when the guard and the driver left for a drink he mounted the footplate. With a saucy 'Toot-toot!' the little train chuffed away – just for fun!

Cornfields, herds of cattle, hills and tunnels; sudden glimpses of blue sea; all these flashed by.

"Da-da-da- – dah!" went the train over the rails, speeding down the slopes, delighted with its light load.

Bobby was whistling. He was a driver at last and this train was his whole world. He noticed the rust on the railway lines.

'Oh dear,' he thought, 'they should be gleaming bright.' He didn't know the engine had been switched onto an old disused set of rails.

The little engine knew things weren't quite right and slowed down as it came to another tunnel. There, earth, boulders and rocks had spread right across the track. Bobby was disappointed; it was impossible to go on.

He got down and found there was room for him to squeeze through. He went into the tunnel. It was very dark in there, except for a small round patch of light in the far distance, where the tunnel ended. He didn't get to the end, for about half-way, a large cave opened into the hillside. There, hanging on the walls were lots of tiny, shining lamps.

Low work-benches were under each light and small tools laid out in neat rows. Pebbles were in piles; some dull, others smooth and shiny. Further into the cave, Bobby saw daylight pouring in through a slit in the wall. Looking through it, he could see right down to the sandy beach.

Then he saw them: six little men, heads down, scraping the sand. They were thin, quite old with white hair and beards, but quick and active. Each had an apron tied round his middle. They popped things into their pockets as they worked.

Suddenly they all stopped and came towards the cave.

'This must be their workshop,' thought Bobby and he hid in the darkest corner.

In they came and tipped their treasure into one big basket; minute shells – small enough to make dainty necklaces. Some of them started to thread needles with silk; others took a handful of shells to polish. They hummed as they worked, but not a word was spoken.

Bobby was very interested. He was also very hungry and felt in his knapsack for his sandwiches. He was munching away and still watching when the little men lifted their heads, took a deep breath and searched all round the cave by sniffing.

They found him and stood looking – not so much at him, as at his food. Bobby offered the packet; there was just one sandwich each. The little men thanked him with smiles, sat down near him and ate. He shared his bag of cookies with them and when he opened a chocolate bar, they laughed with delight. He had to show them his empty knapsack to prove he had nothing left.

They took him round to the benches and understood when he asked about their work. They showed him what they were doing, but no one spoke a word. One finished a necklace while Bobby looked on, and with a shy smile gave it to him, slipping it into his pocket. Bobby found them each a glass marble, curved with pretty colours which pleased them very much.

Then they beckoned him and led him down a narrow passage. Down and down it went, deep into the earth, the way lit by more tiny lamps. Steps and still more steps, and there they were – under the sea . . . in a huge tank with walls and ceiling the colour of glass . . . the pale green light of the water moving all round them. Bobby could see beautiful plants growing on the rocks outside, opening and closing, waving their leaves and branches. Shoals of brightly coloured fish gazed in at them. The little men enjoyed showing their special place to Bobby. They laughed and giggled when he kept saying how wonderful it was.

When a large fish touched the glass with its nose, Bobby was glad to be inside.

'We're like goldfish in a bowl' he thought, 'and they are like people outside.'

Suddenly the pale light was in deep shadow. Something was resting above . . . A ship? . . . Bobby heard the clink of a chain . . . If an anchor came down and broke the roof they would all drown!

Bobby cried out and pointed up, explaining what might happen, but his friends didn't understand the danger. Seeing an anchor lowering straight down onto them, he grabbed two of the little men and raced towards the narrow passage. Pushing them up the steps, he shouted:

"We'll be flooded! . . . Hurry! . . . I'll get the others!"

He doubled back, rounded up the other four, and holding one by his beard, pushed them out of the cave as the anchor clanked down. It made a ghastly sound and the glass cracked!

In seconds, the roof would collapse under the pressure of water. Bobby half-carried the little men up the steps. Breathlessly he said,

"Go on! . . . Be quick! . . . Hurry! . . . The water's coming!"

It seemed hours before they reached the top. When they looked down, the dark, surging water was splashing over the bottom steps.

The little men knew then why Bobby had handled them so roughly. They patted his hands and tried to smile. They were sad about their lost room under the sea, and shocked to think of the dreadful end they had escaped.

Back in the big cave, they all sat down for a rest. They needed it after their race against the sea.

Bobby came out of his sleep to hear a 'Toot — Toot' from the little engine. He looked round to say goodbye to his friends, but they had gone back to their search for shells. There was no time to look for them; he must take the train back to the station.

The engine was ready to be off. Bobby backed the engine away for some distance to switch it onto the right rails. At the station he climbed up into the same carriage he had travelled in that morning.

The children came trailing in from their happy, tiring day. All were counted and checked and soon they were on their way home.

"Da-da-da- dah!" sang the little train and the children nodded sleepily.

"I didn't see you on the beach, Bobby," said one teacher. "Did you have a good day?"

"Yes, thank you," said Bobby. "The most exciting day I've ever had."

"You'll be able to write a good story about it then," she smiled.

Bobby smiled too, holding the shell necklace in his pocket.

'They wouldn't believe it if I did!' he thought.

THE PRINCESS AND THE PARASOL

What present would Princess Sing Cha Lu want for her tenth birthday? Everyone in the kingdom of Tai Tuan was waiting to know. If the Princess wanted a golden necklace, goldsmiths would work night and day making fine golden chains to give the Princess her wish. If she wanted a string of pearls, the best divers in Tai Tuan would search for hours for the largest pearls they could find in the ocean. If Princess Sing Cha Lu wanted a dress of peacock feathers, seamstresses would sew from dawn till dusk to make it for her. The people of Tai Tuan loved their King and Queen and they would do anything for the young Princess, but indeed Princess Sing Cha Lu was very spoilt.

When she made her servants race through the market, pulling her rickshaw as fast as it would go, Sing Cha Lu would squeal with delight. Stalls were knocked to the ground and fruit and flowers trampled underfoot. "Never mind," the people would say. "One day, little Sing Cha Lu will grow into a fine Princess."

When the Princess walked to the rice fields with her pet dogs, she let them run among the growing shoots. The rice crops were ruined. "Never mind," the people would say. "One day, little Sing Cha Lu will grow into a fine Princess."

Every year, the people of Tai Tuan had a holiday. It was the day of the Great Festival. In the morning they rested. Then a sampan race was held. Sampans are small boats used in China. In the evening, everyone would enjoy a grand display of fireworks.

The King had a surprise for his daughter, which was a magic gift. It was a delicate parasol, studded with tiny green jewels. How fine Sing Cha Lu would look riding to the Festival with her beautiful parasol. When the Princess raised it above her head and made a wish, she had power over the Sun, the Rain and the Clouds. She could make the day warm or cold, sunny or cloudy. Princess Sing Cha Lu had never felt so important in her whole life.

In the afternoon, everyone watched the sampan race. What fun it was. The people laughed with pleasure as they placed bets on the winner.

Just then, the Princess opened her parasol. The sun disappeared behind the clouds and strong winds began to blow. The little boats bobbed on the waves and were swept out to sea. The sampan race was spoilt, which made everyone sad. But there were still the fireworks to enjoy.

When the storm died down and the evening sky grew dark, crowds gathered to see the great display. As it began, fountains of colour streaked across the sky; the Princess opened her parasol. At once, there was a cloudburst, so heavy that all the fireworks were put out. Cold, wet and very upset, the people went back home. Some of them asked, "Do you think that little Sing Cha Lu will ever grow into a fine Princess?"

As Sing Cha Lu's birthday drew near, everyone waited to hear what birthday present she would choose. The Princess took a walk in the Palace gardens to decide what she would ask from her father.

'How lovely I would look in a gown of peacock feathers,' she thought. 'Maybe I could bind my long hair with a fine golden chain . . .'

It was cool in the gardens and Sing Cha Lu raised her parasol to make the sun come out. To her great surprise, the parasol turned inside out. A great gust of wind lifted her high into the air. She held on to the parasol tightly as it sailed over the Palace walls and away.

Sing Cha Lu shouted angrily,

"What is the meaning of this? I am the Princess of Tai Tuan. Parasol, you must let me down at once!"

Then she heard strange voices saying,

"We are the spirits of Earth and Air, of Sky and Water; we may take you where we will." The Princess Sing Cha Lu was afraid.

"But I don't want to fly through the air," she cried, and tried to stamp her little foot! Oh dear! She almost lost her hold on the parasol.

"It's not fair," she cried. "I want to go home!" The earth looked so far away and she felt very near to tears.

Soon the Princess and the parasol were flying over the mountains; far below she saw a small wooden house. Seated outside was a girl of her own age, very thin and pale.

"Who is that little girl?" she asked. "I would call to her for help, but she looks very silly to me."

The Spirit of Air answered in a silvery voice, which made Sing Cha Lu tremble:

"That girl is not well. She leaves her mountain home only once a year for the great Firework Festival – but if you remember, this year it was spoilt by rain."

"I expect she was as cross as cross could be," said Sing Cha Lu.

"Oh no," said the Spirit of Air. "I did not hear her complain."

Swiftly the wind lifted the Princess and the parasol higher into the air and they sailed across the sky towards the sea. On the shore below, Sing Cha Lu could see an old man mending his boat.

"What is he doing?" she asked.

The Spirit of Water bubbled and gurgled and said, in a voice which made Sing Cha Lu tremble, "His boat was wrecked in the storm during the Festival Race and it will take days to mend it."

"Was he very angry?" Sing Cha Lu whispered.

"Oh no," answered the Spirit of Water. "I did not hear him complain."

Sing Cha Lu could not think of anything to say, but now there were tears in her eyes as the wind blew the parasol inland again.

Soon they were over the Palace grounds and as the Princess floated back to the ground, the wind snatched the parasol from her fingers. Weaving and gliding through the air, it disappeared far, far away over the mountains.

Sing Cha Lu watched until it was out of sight, then she ran to the Palace and called the King.

"Father, I would like three things for my birthday, please."

The King's heart fell. Would he have to ask the goldsmiths AND the divers AND the seamstresses to work day and night for Sing Cha Lu's gifts?

"What would you like, my child?" he asked.

Sing Cha Lu explained, "I would like my birthday to be a holiday for everyone in Tai Tuan. We could have a great sampan race, with prizes for the winners, and in the evening, the best fireworks display ever."

The King looked in wonder at his little daughter. "Would those things make your birthday a happy day, my child?"

"Oh yes, Father," replied Princess Sing Cha Lu. "I would like everyone to be happy with me."

When the people of Tai Tuan heard about the birthday plans, some of them said, "I told you so" and others said, "Well, I never." But they all agreed, "Why, now we can say that our little Sing Cha Lu has grown into a fine Princess."

THE DANCING SHOES

Midge was a very naughty little elf. He spent his day playing tricks on people. He often got into trouble but this did not make any difference. He just could not stop himself, even though at times, he did try.

He was standing in Mr Merryweather's shoe store one afternoon, when there came a loud tap-tapping at the door. Mr Merryweather went to see who was there. He found an officer of the king's guard standing outside, holding a very large letter. The officer handed it to Mr Merryweather who opened and read it.

Then, a strange thing happened. Mr Merryweather jumped, kicking his heels in the air and danced all round the store.

Then he took Midge's hand and shook it warmly.

"Would you believe it," he said beaming. "The king has asked me to make him a pair of shoes. Just think, *me* making shoes for the king!"

Midge smiled at Mr Merryweather. At the same time he felt a tingling in his fingertips, a feeling he often had when he was about to do something naughty.

That evening, Midge sat at home looking into the fire, turning over all kinds of ideas in his mind. Then he found he could not sit still any longer, so he went outside.

The moon was full and countless stars twinkled overhead, but Midge did not see because he was too busy thinking.

He wandered through the streets and stopped outside Mr Merryweather's store. There was a new sign hanging in the window, it read,

    M. MERRYWEATHER
SHOEMAKER TO HIS MAJESTY
        THE KING

Midge thought of the new shoes and smiled to himself. Walking round to the back of the store, he noticed that one of the windows was slightly open. By carefully working at the catch, Midge managed to open it and climb inside.

On the counter, he saw a fine pair of red shoes with large golden buckles. He knew that they must be the new shoes for the king. Looking around, he also saw on a shelf, a box with a label which read, NAILS FOR DANCING SHOES.

An idea came into his head. Carefully Midge took the box down from the shelf. He picked up a hammer and began to knock some of the nails into one of the red shoes. When he had finished, he put everything back into place and crept back silently to his house.

The next morning, a guardsman called upon Mr Merryweather for the shoes. Mr Merryweather wrapped them carefully and the guardsman left, taking them with him.

When the king saw the shoes, he was delighted.

"They are just what I wanted," he said, putting them on.

He looked in the mirror, and as he did so, the king gave a funny little skip. He took the shoes off and handed them to his servant, saying that he would wear them to the banquet later that evening.

The king had invited many important people to the palace. He was very pleased that he would be able to show off his new shoes.

When everyone was seated that evening and dinner was about to be served, the king felt his feet begin to twitch. At first, he tried not to take any notice. The twitching in his feet became worse and the king just had to get up and dance. The important people at the table looked on as the king jigged all around the room, his coat-tails flying out behind him. They stared and whispered, but the poor king could not stop dancing.

The dance went on for an hour until the king stopped at last, and sank wearily onto his throne.

"Quickly," he shouted, "take these shoes off before they make me start again."

The king was very angry at being made to look like a fool. He ordered that the shoes be burnt. The guard thought that the shoes were too good to burn. He took them outside the palace gates and left them there.

The shoes lay there for two days before a girl from the village found them. She thought how grand she would look in them, so putting them on, she skipped off to school.

In the middle of a lesson, the girl felt her feet begin to twitch and her toes tap a little tune. Suddenly, she jumped up from her seat and danced round the classroom.

The teacher shouted at her to sit down, but the girl went on dancing. Thinking that she was just being silly, the teacher became very angry. When the girl stopped dancing, he told her to stay in the classroom after school and write one hundred times, I MUST NOT DANCE IN SCHOOL.

On her way home, the girl threw the shoes away.

Old Mrs Maguire on her way to market, was the next person to find the shoes. There they were, lying half hidden by a hedge. Her own shoes were worn and old. Mrs Maguire could not believe her luck at finding new ones. Putting them on, she hobbled on her way.

She had walked only a few steps when her feet began to twitch. She gave a little skip, then another and the shoes were off dancing again.

The people in the village were very surprised to see Mrs Maguire kicking her heels in the air and dancing in the street. Everyone stopped and stared. The poor old lady tried calling out for help, but no one could run fast enough to catch up with her.

When at last the shoes stopped, a very tired Mrs Maguire sank into a heap in the middle of the road.

"Quickly," called someone. "Fetch a doctor!"

The doctor came, carrying a large bag from which he took a small green bottle which he held under Mrs Maguire's nose. The old lady sneezed and then said in a shaky voice, "It's the shoes. Please, please take them off."

The doctor removed the shoes and looked at them carefully. Since he was a boy, the doctor had taken an interest in magic. He knew at once that there was something funny about the shoes. He placed them on the ground and said, "Go and find the one who started all this."

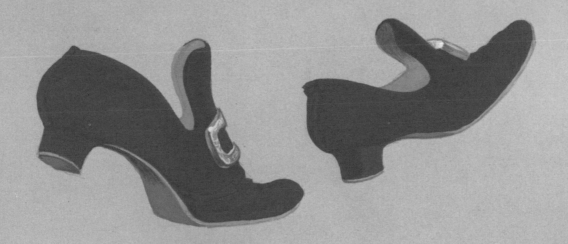

The shoes gave a little skip all by themselves and danced to a spot behind the wall, where Midge lay curled up like a ball, shaking with laughter.

The shoes slipped onto his feet and danced him back to the doctor.

"I might have known that you were the cause of the mischief," the doctor said, glaring down at him. "Now let us see how well *you* dance."

Midge felt his feet twitch and he started to dance. He could not stop. Down the street he danced, while everyone clapped and cheered. Out of the village and over the hills he danced. And that was the last the village people ever saw of Midge, the naughty elf.

WIZARD BEANIE

In those far off days in 'once upon a time' land there lived a good kind wizard. He was called Wizard Beanie because he was so tall and thin that he looked like a bean pole.

Now the house where he lived was almost a ruin and everyone told him he should do something about it. But Wizard Beanie never seemed to have the time.

"Why don't you magic yourself a new house?" someone asked him.

"What a good idea, I never thought of it," said the wizard.

He looked up all his old spells but the only one he could find was for making a palace and that would be much too big for him. So he set to work to make his own spell. Then he put on his hat, nodded his head three times, waved his wand and hey presto, the ruin disappeared and a house stood there instead.

But there was one thing wrong with it. The house wasn't high enough for Wizard Beanie. He was bent almost double and could not stand up at all. Thinking he had made a mistake, he did the spell again but the same thing happened.

He crawled out of the door and straightened himself. He could see over the roof top easily.

Wizard Beanie scratched his head. Now what was he to do? It looked a good strong house. It would be warm and dry in the winter, but it was no use to him as he would be most uncomfortable bent double all day.

Then he had an idea and chuckling to himself, he crawled back in and worked another spell.

At once the spell began to work; he could feel himself shrinking and in no time at all he could stand up quite comfortably in his new home. But now instead of being like a bean pole he was short and fat. Yes, – fat! That was something he wasn't expecting but luckily his clothes stretched so he did not burst out of them. One other thing had gone wrong too, but he did not know about that yet.

Some of the people from the village had noticed the new house and had come to look at it.

"Not very high, is it?" said one.

"How on earth is Wizard Beanie going to stand up in there?" asked another.

Wizard Beanie smiled to himself and went out to greet them.

Everyone stared at him in amazement.

"Hello," he greeted them.

"Who are you?" one of them asked.

"Who am I? Wizard Beanie, of course," he answered looking surprised.

A crowd had gathered by now and they started muttering.

"What have you done with our wizard?" one shouted.

"Yes," threatened the crowd. "What have you done with him?"

"But I *am* Beanie," protested the puzzled wizard. "I have only made myself smaller to fit my new house."

"Wizard Beanie had black hair, yours is red," called out a little boy.

"Red? Good heavens!" gasped Beanie. "Are you sure?"

"Of course we are sure," retorted an old dame. "Look." She handed him a small mirror.

"Thank you Mary," said the Wizard. "How is your rheumatism today?"

Then he looked into the mirror and he had such a shock. His hair was indeed red and he did not look like himself at all.

"Oh well," he admitted. "I suppose I cannot blame you for being suspicious when I look like this."

"Well John," he said looking at the man next to him. "Is Daisy the cow better today? And you, Frank. How is your wife now? Feeling alright again?"

The people gazed at him. How did he know them all if he wasn't Wizard Beanie? Then he started to laugh and he was so fat he shook like a jelly.

"The trouble is," he chuckled. "My spells never seem to work for myself. Anyway, I must do something to look like my old self again."

He went back into the new house and when he came out the crowd gasped. His hair was black again and he wasn't half as fat.

"Ah, that feels better," he sighed. "Do I look more like myself now?"

Everybody laughed and cheered. They gathered around him to touch him or clap him on the back.

"You are still plump," said Mary. "Or perhaps I should say portly."

"We can't call you Beanie anymore," said Frank.

"I think I would rather be portly than look like a bean pole," smiled the wizard.

"We will call you Wizard Portly then," laughed John.

"Hip-hip-hurray for Wizard Portly," shouted the children.

Everyone cheered loudly and they were all happy again in 'once upon a time' land.

GLUM THE GIANT

Glum, the Giant, strode along the road away from the village with his bag on his shoulder. He had been shopping. Several people smiled at him but he only nodded back at them. They took no notice, they were used to him.

Then some children followed him chanting,
"There goes poor old Glum,
He has a pain in his tum.
Oh, why does he scowl?
He should be called Growl."

Glum spun round and glared at them. They ran away laughing, as they knew he would not harm them.

Glum went on his way thinking hard. What was the matter with him? Why couldn't he smile and laugh like other people? Perhaps if he tried it would help. How did they smile? They showed their teeth, didn't they? Glum thought he would try out his idea of a smile on the next person he saw.

The giant went on his way until he saw a boy on a horse coming towards him.

"Hello Glum," called the boy. Glum remembered his idea and smiled. At least he thought it was a smile, but it frightened the horse so much that it reared up and bolted almost unseating the boy.

Glum dropped his bag and took only a few strides to catch the horse by the reins, just in time.

"Whoa there," Glum said gently stroking the horse's nose with one finger while he helped the boy to sit up straight. The horse stopped trembling and neighed as if in answer.

"Are you alright, boy?" he asked.

"Yes, thank you," was the rather shaky answer.

"Well, take it easy then, goodbye."

Glum left the boy wondering what could have happened for the giant to pull such a funny face.

Glum came to a large pond where a lot of ducks and fish lived. He leaned over to look into the water but his shadow was so dark that he could not see himself.

Glum still did not know what he looked like.

He carried on until he came to his gloomy old castle and went in slamming the door behind him.

Glum looked about him and seemed to see everything with new eyes. He had never noticed before that the dark grey walls were hanging with cobwebs, or that the floor was so dirty and the furniture thick with dust. He had no one to look after him, it was true.

"That is no excuse," Glum told himself, suddenly upset with the state the place was in.

"I ought to look for a wife, but who would have me? If the castle has to be cleaned I will have to do it myself."

He made himself some supper and went to bed feeling more glum than ever.

That night he had a strange dream. He was a handsome giant who had rescued a fair young giantess from the clutches of her wicked uncle. When he woke he remembered his dream and thought sadly how lonely he was.

"Come on," he reminded himself. "There is work to be done."

All day long he swept, dusted and polished the old castle. Clouds of dust flew out of the doors and all the windows. The people in the village some distance away wondered what on earth was happening.

By the time Glum had finished, the castle looked a different place but he himself was a mess; not that he ever looked very tidy but now he was dirty as well.

He picked up a large bar of soap and a towel as big as a blanket and made his way to the river nearby.

First, he took off his boots, emptied the dust out of them, then polished them with his sleeve until they shone. Then he waded into the river as he was, with his clothes on and sat in the middle of it.

"Ah," he sighed. "That feels nice and cool after all my hard work."

Glum bent forward to splash himself with water, holding the soap in one hand. He stared at the face looking back at him for a few moments, then he began to roar with peals of laughter. He laughed and laughed until the tears rolled down his cheeks.

At last, still chuckling, he looked up to see the people from the village standing on the bank watching him in amazement.

"Are you alright?" one of the men asked him.

Glum laughed again.

"I've just seen the funniest face looking up at me from the river," he explained. "It is the first time I have seen something that made me want to laugh. I do feel good now. I can understand at last why people like to smile and feel happy."

"That was your own face in the water," one little boy said before they could stop him.

"My own face?" Glum sounded astonished. He looked again into the water and saw himself once more.

"Well," he said at last. "If that is what I look like, no wonder I am called Glum."

He put his head under the water and gave himself a good scrub, clothes and all. Then he stood up and shook himself before reaching for his towel.

''I can cut your hair and trim your beard if you would like me to,'' the barber dared to say.

''Why, that is most kind of you,'' Glum said smiling at him.

They all smiled back.

''No time like the present,'' the barber said, taking comb and scissors from his pocket.

When he had finished, everybody stared at Glum.

''There, that has made a difference, hasn't it?'' said the barber.

Glum leaned over and looked at himself in the river. He turned his head from side to side, putting his hand up to feel his beard. Then he smiled and at last he laughed showing his white teeth. His hair and beard were brown and his eyes deep blue.

"Is that really me?" he asked.

"Yes, indeed it is," an old lady answered. "If I may say so, you are a very handsome giant now."

Glum rose to his feet and bowed low to her. "Thank you, my lady," he chuckled.

Everybody clapped and laughed. The children danced around him singing,

"Oh me, oh my, what a handsome guy,

He will make all the ladies sigh."

Then Glum thought, maybe some day, his dream might not be so impossible after all.

141

THE IMPATIENT WITCH

Flewella the Witch was worried,
Her pet frogs had all jumped away,
Her cauldron had rusted completely,
And her bats had flown to Bombay.

A black cat had swallowed her spiders,
And her broomstick had snapped in half,
Her rats were all playing Bingo,
And her crow was asleep in the bath.

"I'm getting too old," she said sadly,
"I'm wrinkled and losing my brain,
I'll visit the local Witch Doctor,
He'll magic me young again."

The Witch Doctor listened intently,
And mixed her a bright yellow brew,
"A sip a day for a week," he said,
"And avoid carrots, doughnuts and stew."

142

Now Flewella was very impatient,
She swallowed the brew in one go,
Then she settled down in the armchair,
To wait for the magic to show.

But the potion worked very quickly,
In fact, by a quarter to four,
Flewella was sitting like a baby,
Clapping her hands, on the floor.

"She should have followed instructions,"
The Witch Doctor said, aghast,
"A sipful a day, not a bottle,
No wonder it worked so fast!"

Flewella giggled and gurgled,
And waved her bottle aloft,
She stayed like that for a couple of weeks,
Until the magic wore off!

143

A PIG CALLED FANCY

Fancy, the blue pig, opened one eye and peered down through the branches of the big green tree in which he lived. He rustled his wings a little in his cosy nest and then shivered, partly because it was still early in the morning and a little cold, and partly from excitement. Today was the day when he was going on his adventure.

For a long time now, almost since he could remember anything, Fancy had been trying to find out why he was blue and had wings. All the other pigs he knew were pink and lived on the ground. Everyone who met him said "Fancy, a blue pig," until in the end, that was all anyone called him. Fancy didn't know whether he had ever had another name.

He uncurled himself a little further and peered over the edge of his snug home. It was a very long way up in the tree, but that was one of the best things about it, he thought. No one laughed at him up there. The only creatures he talked to were the birds. They took it for granted that anything that lived in a tree could fly. They thought there wasn't anything different at all about Fancy.

The fat little pig clambered out of his nest and unfolded his wings. They were not feathery like a bird's, they were rather silky and very thin, so that when Fancy flew, the sun shone through them and made them sparkle with all the colours of the rainbow. Even though the other pigs laughed at Fancy, he was very proud of his wings.

Avoiding the branches of his tree and the other tall trees nearby, Fancy glided down to earth. He landed with only a little bump.

He was much better at it than he used to be. When he first began to fly, he couldn't manage to land properly at all. He came down with a terrific crash, which left him quite bruised and breathless. Sometimes, he forgot to fold his wings in time, so that he kept bouncing up and down instead of staying on the ground. But now, he was really good. He zoomed in for a superb landing and started looking for breakfast. He snuffled around on the carpet of leaves, looking for nuts and berries. He knew it was very important to eat well before he left on his adventure. After all, who knew where he would be when it came to his next mealtime.

He had a large breakfast and set off. He went North. A long time ago, when Fancy was very small indeed, a visitor had arrived in the forest. He was not like anything anyone had ever seen. He was, everyone supposed, a Cat, but his fur had been bright green. His eyes were gold and glittered when he spoke. The other animals were a little afraid of him, but Fancy had liked him and asked, at once, if the Cat could help him solve his problem.

The golden eyes had glittered, the fur had gleamed greenly in the sunshine and Cat had said, ''Go North, that is where your answer lies.'' Fancy wasn't too good at directions, as he was very young, but he remembered what Cat said. When he was old enough, he had decided that North was where he would go.

He tramped through the forest, deciding to fly when the trees had thinned out a little. The sun could barely reach through the thick forest. Fancy had to keep moving in order to stay warm. The animals he met all seemed busy and not very friendly. There was a snake which hung down from a branch on a tree and gazed at him without speaking. Fancy hurried past — he didn't care for the way the snake was looking at him. Perhaps snakes ate pigs, even blue ones with wings.

A bird with golden red feathers fluttered by. He looked more friendly and so Fancy said, "Excuse me, but am I going North?"

The bird stopped for a moment and gazed at Fancy. "North? Indeed! Why yes, that's the place for you." Then he hurried on. Fancy had begun to feel a little more cheerful when there was a thundering noise behind him. In his fright, he flapped his wings and flew up to the nearest branch where he huddled, very still.

A beautiful white horse thundered through the forest. Fancy looked down as it slowed to a canter beneath his tree. It wasn't a proper horse at all, he thought, for he could see that it had a horn on its forehead. It was . . . it really was a Unicorn. Fancy had heard about Unicorns but he had never thought he would see one. The Unicorn slowed to a walk and it looked up into the tree.

"What are you doing on that branch, little blue pig?" it breathed at Fancy, rather than spoke. Fancy was so scared he nearly fell off his branch. Plucking up all his courage he spoke to the huge animal.

"Where I live all the pigs are pink and they laugh at me. I like to fly and I am proud of my wings, but I want to know why I am different. The Cat that came to our forest said I must go North and that is what I am trying to do."

"Come with me, little pig — I too, travel North. You may ride on my back if you think you can stay there," said the Unicorn.

"Oh yes, please," squeaked Fancy. Never in his life had he dreamed of such adventure. To ride on a Unicorn's back. Together they sped through the forest. Fancy had to spread his wings a little now and then to keep his balance, but he managed very well.

Before Fancy knew what had happened, the forest had come to an end. At last he knew why everyone had told him to go North. Before him lay a valley — the sun shone and the grass was green. In the distance a river sparkled and gleamed, small green-furred cats played on the ground and the air was full, just full of blue pigs, with wings of silk which rustled and shone in the light.

Without a backward glance Fancy took off from the Unicorn's back. He was home at last!

148

MISS POLLYWOBBLE

Miss Pollywobble put another log on the fire and watched it blaze merrily away. It was a bitterly cold evening and Baggy, her ginger cat sat very close to the fire. Outside, the snow started to fall and by bedtime, the countryside was covered by a huge, white snowy blanket.

"We haven't many logs left," said Miss Pollywobble the next morning, as she gave Baggy his milk and sardines for breakfast. "I've ordered some from the village. Maybe they will come today."

Baggy purred happily and tucked into his food.

But the snow continued to fall steadily and almost covered the cottage. Miss Pollywobble and Baggy began to feel very cold. They had run out of logs and none could be delivered because the roads were blocked by snowdrifts.

Miss Pollywobble wore two dresses, three cardigans, a woolly hat and a pair of big, fur boots. She ate hot soup and toast and managed to keep warm. Baggy stopped purring altogether and shivered miserably. He snuggled up to Miss Pollywobble to keep warm.

"Poor Baggy," she said, cuddling him close to her. "Let's find you a blanket." She opened the cupboard and out fell a big bag of wool.

After staring at it thoughtfully for some time she said, "I've just had the most marvellous idea, Baggy. I shall knit something to keep us both warm."

She found a large pair of knitting needles and made herself comfortable. All day and all night she clicked away as the knitting grew bigger and bigger. At last it was finished. It was enormous!

Baggy was very puzzled. He watched as Miss Pollywobble went outside carrying her largest broom. She pulled a ladder out from under the snow and climbed up onto the roof. Then she swept every bit of snow from the walls and roof until they were spotlessly clean. She then returned indoors to fetch the 'marvellous idea' and climbed the ladder again. With a few tugs and a few pulls the knitting fell into place.

Baggy blinked hard.

Miss Pollywobble had knitted a gigantic red tea cosy! It fitted the cottage perfectly. The hole for the handle was over the front door and the hole for the spout was over the back door. The chimney poked through the red pom-poms on the top.

It was a little dark inside the
cottage but it was beautifully warm.
Baggy snuggled down happily and
Miss Pollywobble took off her big,
fur boots. They were warm inside
their giant tea cosy and didn't mind
at all when it began to snow again.

It snowed steadily for days. One
morning, Miss Pollywobble woke up
to find the cottage strangely light
and extremely cold. She quickly
flung open the window.

"Baggy!" she cried, sadly. "Our
tea cosy! It's disappeared!"

Baggy shivered sadly. Miss Pollywobble looked hard at the
snow-covered countryside. Whoever had taken the giant tea cosy had
been very careful indeed! The snow was smooth and there were no
footprints. She closed the window thoughtfully and went downstairs.

She warmed some milk for Baggy's breakfast and made herself some
coffee. Birds twittered noisily on the window ledge. Miss Pollywobble
always gave them breadcrumbs for breakfast and she scattered a handful
from the window. As she did so, she saw something flapping gently in the
snowy hedge. It was an end of red wool!

"Come on, Baggy," she cried, pulling on her snow shoes. "We're going
to follow that wool!"

She put Baggy into her shopping basket and they set off. The red wool trailed over fields and farms and along narrow lanes. After many, many miles they came to a dark, gloomy forest. A square, wooden sign said,

KNITTINGHAM FOREST. KEEP OUT.

The trail of wool led deep into the forest and then stopped suddenly. Miss Pollywobble looked all around while Baggy started digging with his front paws and then jumped back in alarm.

He had found an old underground tunnel and the red wool continued along it.

Bravely Miss Pollywobble made her way into the tunnel and Baggy came slowly behind. It was damp and dark and silent. The wool led them on until they come to a big brown door. They could hear lots of squeaky voices chattering inside.

Miss Pollywobble took a deep breath and slowly opened the door.

Inside was a large, bright room full of small, elf-like creatures. They wore green, knitted clothes and all looked alike. The floor was covered with balls of wool and everyone was busy knitting with the tiniest needles Miss Pollywobble had ever seen. Everyone became very, very quiet.

"Please don't be afraid,' she said, gently. "I'm Miss Pollywobble, and this is my cat, Baggy. We followed the trail of red wool from our giant tea cosy. Please tell us who you are."

Then one of the elf-like creatures stepped forward.

"We are the Knit Wits," he said. "We live here in Knittingham Forest and spend all our time knitting."

153

"But what do you knit?" asked Miss Pollywobble. The Knit Wit led her across the room to some small drawers neatly stacked together. In the top drawer there were lots of tiny yellow, knitted tubes.

"In the very cold weather," explained the Knit Wit, "the catkins in the forest would freeze. We knit little covers to keep them warm."

Miss Pollywobble smiled. "What a lovely idea," she said.

The rest of the Knit Wits gathered round to show off their knitting. There were tiny red vests for the robins and pretty yellow hats for the daffodils, and long ear muffs for rabbits. There were bluebell covers and white snowdrop covers. In fact, every living thing in Knittingham Forest had something warm for the winter.

Miss Pollywobble liked the Knit Wits very much. "How kind you are," she said, gently.

One of them touched her arm. "We're so sorry we undid your giant tea cosy," he said, "but our red wool was stolen and we needed some new vests for the robins."

A loud tapping on the door made everyone jump.

"It's Colonel Crow!" cried the Knit Wits. "He's the one who stole all our red wool to make himself a warm nest. Quick, Miss Pollywobble, hide in the wool cupboard!"

The door suddenly burst open. "We've no more wool for you, Colonel Crow," said a Knit Wit. "If you leave us alone we will knit you a new nest. Please go away."

But the Crow took no notice and started gathering wool from the floor.

The Knit Wits huddled together in a corner. Colonel Crow was the nastiest Crow they had ever met and they were very frightened.

Then, the door of the wool cupboard burst open with a crash and out sprang Baggy, looking very angry. Colonel Crow, dropped all the wool and with a startled "Caw" ran to the tunnel. Baggy chased him out into the daylight and through Knittingham Forest. He made sure that Colonel Crow flew far, far away.

The Knit Wits were delighted and thanked Baggy over and over again. Miss Pollywobble picked him up and popped him in her basket once more. Then she said goodbye to each Knit Wit and promised to visit them again soon.

The sun was shining as they walked across the fields. The trees began to drip as the snow started to melt. When they arrived home they were happy to find their logs had arrived at last and were stacked neatly against the wall of the cottage. Baggy purred happily at the thought of a blazing log fire.

Some days later, Miss Pollywobble found a large brown paper parcel on the doorstep. She opened it very carefully and found a pink, knitted vest for herself and a ginger knitted coat for Baggy. She smiled fondly. She knew exactly who had sent them!